Random Highs

Written by

Abir Chanan El

43rdbooks.com

Random Highs

Written by

Abir Chanan El

43rdbooks.com

© 2021

Califa Media Publishing ™

Lafayette, IN

ISBN-13: 978-1-952828-11-9

Other Titles

by Abir Chanan El

Love is a Privilege, Not a Guarantee: A Survivor
Manual for Relationships

The Game is Timeless

Knower's Ark: The Travels of Dante the Dredlock

Visit Abir online at 43rdBooks.com

Table of Contents

PROLOGUE

Random

> *Definition: a person or thing that is unknown, unidentified, or suspiciously out of place.*

> *Slang: a person or thing that is odd or unpredictable.*

Highs

> *Definition: a notable happy or successful moment; a state of euphoria.*

CHAPTER 1

"... Love and drugs, drugs and Love ..."

This is Jorge Freeman, News Chopper 7, Afternoon Report. We're live from Old Dred Bridge where things have gotten intense. For the past hour and a half, a young lady has seemingly been thinking about leaping off the 150-foot bridge.

From what we can tell, this 20-something, brown-skinned woman drove to the top of this bridge, used her Dodge Intrepid to block both northbound lanes, jumped from her vehicle, and hopped onto the railings of this historic bridge. We are a good distance from her now, but thanks to some great camera work, we can tell she has two items with her: one in her hand, which seems to be a cell phone, and another unidentifiable object protruding from the side pocket of her pink Abercrombie hoodie.

Of course, we all want this young lady to make it out of here alive, but what a crazy time to stage this. It's Labor Day weekend and Old Dred Bridge is the gateway to this area's beaches. So, it goes without saying that countless motorists are peeved that traffic is completely gridlocked at least seven to eight miles back.

Law enforcement could not cut through the traffic, so were forced to drive southward up the northbound lanes to reach this young lady's position. About ten minutes ago, they sent out an officer of some sort, maybe a negotiator, to open communications with this desperate young lady. We'll stay right here Monument City until we figure out what's going on further. I'm Jorge Freeman, New Chopper 7.

—

"Oooweee!!! It's hotter than a witch's teat out here, ain't it?" the officer joked. "Funny, yaknow? I've lived here my whole damn life and I ain't neva' stood atop of dis here bridge. WOW! It's beautiful, ain't it? Scary as all hell too."

The young lady never parted lips, just picked up her phone, punched in a text or something, and set it back down on her lap. Her hazel eyes stared into the distant waters. Her posture was perfect, not slumping at all. She's totally collected, and other than her rocking her legs back and forth over the railing, she didn't appear scared or even anxious for that matter.

"Well uh, hey, you gotta name, lil' lady?" he asked.

She hunched her shoulders aggressively and growled, "Bruh! does it look like I want to be bothered right now?"

"Whoa! Whoa! Aye! Okay, lil' lady! I hear you. Well uh, do you smoke by chance? Hell, I do. I know I shouldn't, but hell sometimes nothing calms me down better than a good ole' cigarette?" he said.

"Mane damn! YES! I think I will 'toke' one, but I only smoke Newport's, and I brought my own pack," she said becoming irritated.

"Great. Who smokes anything else anyway, yaknow?" he said mumbling.

"Only dummies, if you ask me!!" she responded, grabbing a pack from her back pocket. She spanked it, pulled one out with her lips, and lit it.

"Well hey, like I said, a good smoke break always helps everything in my book. Here's to us, lil' lady!" the officer said semi-cheerfully.

Ten minutes go by, he's still talking; she's still speaking only a few words at a time. Suddenly, her phone beeped loudly, a notification of some kind. She checked it quickly as if waiting on someone specifically. Whatever or whomever it was, didn't bring her any relief, as she began to lament loudly.

"Why...do people...keep messing...with me today? DAMN! I just want to be left...THE HELL...ALONE!" she said, cutting her eyes in the officer's direction. That text message obviously shifted her mood quickly. Not only was she irritated now, but the disgruntled drivers stuck on the bridge behind her were getting a little antsy too. Once the motorists realized they were stuck in **traffic**, not just "slow-moving" traffic, all hell broke loose. Barrages of car and truck horns blew like HBCU bands during halftime - so loudly and frequently that some folks got headaches. Then, the cursing and the fighting began. It's like all sudden someone hit a panic button, and that someone's name was Morgan.

Honestly, Morgan could give no "effs" about how everyone else was feeling. It was painfully obvious that she was going through something deep and borderline tragic at that moment. Also, the officer had proven to be useless. All he'd accomplished in the past 30 minutes, was having a cigarette break with a potential suicide victim.

Clumsily, he asked, "Lil' lady, are you waiting on someone specific to get back with you?" The whole mood changed again after his awkward question.

He could have asked anything else, but that question visibly shook her mentally. The sockets around her eyes darkened suddenly like something from a horror flick. She looked sinister, shifting eyes and all. The redbone tone of her face became clammy and lifeless. Her whole aura dropped into a sunken place, and the one person who could fix this situation for her is obviously not responding to her texts. Indeed, everyone involved here was at a crossroads: Morgan, the officer, and the travelers.

Still, Morgan was unbreakable and unmoved as it related to the chaos she was causing. The pain must have been deep. Perhaps, she was too numb from the Prozac pills coupled with her severe depression; it all had her mind twisted horribly like a fat person squeezing in an airplane seat. When she met him, she felt like her life had reached its zenith. Now, his absence had her feeling like she'd been kicked down from the mountaintop, down into the valley again. This is precisely why she hated love and never gave anyone a serious chance. She'd criticized others for so long for sacrificing their happiness to be with someone, now look at her. She thought she'd found a rare man, a rare love to make her rare life purposeful. This was true to a certain extent; she'd found love, but she didn't know how to handle it without being high. Morgan's lifted state of mind constantly pulled in her so many simultaneously conflicting directions that being high or getting toasty were the only foolproof ways for her to deal with everything, especially her love life.

Suddenly, she cried out, "Mane, F*** love. F*** relationships. F*** sex. F*** being high to deal with him. F*** getting high to enjoy sex with him. F*** everything that got to do with him! F*** these dumb asses cursing and blowing their horns at me. I am in the way. I'm in everyone's way. He say I stayed in his way too. Now, he's totally out of my way forever. Love and drugs, drugs and love – what a f***ing combination."

"Young lady, let's talk about this!" the officer shouted in her direction feeling the tension reaching its height." She'd reached the brink of her sanity: no more tolerance, no more compassion, so his voice fell on deaf ears. Slowly sobbing, like someone off that Promethazine, she looked through her phone again, and she waited. The officer waited. The News 7 chopper waited. The thousands behind her waited. Still, no response from anyone, she scooted closer to the edge.

"Wait!!!" the officer screamed. With no more time to think, he rushed her sensing the end was near. Hearing his footsteps scampering towards her quickly, she turned to the officer with tears streaming down her face and said, "I'd rather be with him!"

She leaped off the high railing.

CHAPTER 2

"... Love, Life & The Arts."

Months Later...

My understanding of love changed when I saw my student leap off a 150-foot bridge on live television. Witnessing her tiny body flailing into that river made me realize that I had failed her. Not only her, but I hadn't properly prepared any of my graduating seniors for life and love on a real level.

My name is Esther. Yeah, yeah, I know Esther is an old sounding name, but that's what my mama named me; Esther Bey. Miss Bey-Bey is what they call me around here, and until recently, I was an instructor of a progressive course called Love, Life & Arts at Monument High. In hindsight, I'd have to admit this school year started off with lots of promise; I just wish I would've known the promises would turn catastrophic so quickly.

Monument High school is located deep in the southeast Bayou. The Bayou is an extremely humid, bug-infested swamp that we southerners thoroughly enjoy. Our creeks are filled with 'gators, water moccasins, bullfrogs, crawfish aka crawdads, and other slithering, sneaky unmentionables. Our thick hazy sweltering air is usually too much for those who weren't raised 'round here. And, if the air itself doesn't suffocate ya, then the swarms of gnats, flies, and mosquitoes surely will. "Good!", we the residents of Monument City say, because "if you can't handle the heat, then you shouldn't have ya hind parts in the kitchen."

My Bey family has been here for more generations than any cousin could count. Some folks joke that the Bayou was named after the Bey (aka Bay-ou) family because we've been here for so long. We've owned and still do own several acres of land, including a creek with a forty-foot bridge that separates our two, three-bedroom homes. My parents and I are the last Beys living on the property.

To say it bluntly, the only old thing about me is my name. Monument City is and has been my city since I was a youngen. I've achieved every goal I set my heart to reach by 35 except meeting my king and falling in love. To be honest, I don't need love in my life, but without it people make you feel like you're a homeless, dirty, three-legged mutt.

I don't know why love treats me the way it does. It's crazy because I got the meal, dessert, and all the drippings, yaheard? I'm a 5'4 Creole bilingual gal with olive skin and long black hair that hangs down right above applebum. Woo Chile, got my situation together, so I shouldn't have any problems at all, right? Not true at all!

Anyways, I keep my hair in a bun while I'm teaching my "babies," but during my off hours you can find me somewhere stopping traffic and getting married men in trouble for ogling and eying at this lit-ness. I don't need your opinion; I know I am drop dead gorgeous, and other than this chipped tooth in the front of my mouth I'd be flawless. I have "it." I flaunt "it." Sadly, "it" is my gift and my curse.

The irony is my real gift in life is educating the babies at Monument City high school. My curse, though it sounds crazy to complain about, is I am totally, undeniably, irresistible to all men: single men, married men, young men, old men, just men period. Some women might say - so - how's this a curse? Because it's hard for people to take a gal like me serious when I'm this attractive, other than the chipped tooth of course. The women I work with are jealous and set me up to fail and the men put me into positions where I'll always "owe them something." My students love me because they are in love with me but dammit I have some real life "game" to teach them about Love, Life, and Arts and a short time to do it.

Every quarter, I carefully select eight to twelve students who are interested in taking on a three-hour elective. Most high school seniors are scrambling to graduate, not looking for fun, mind bending classes to add. The first quarter of this year I had eight students the first week. Four students dropped because they weren't mature enough to deal with certain subjects with brutal honesty. For instance, if I ask about teachers propositioning students for sex and sensual favors and a student replies with a funny joke: DENIED!

Some might say that deep questions are above these kids heads at this point. I say these students deal with an onslaught of grown-folk issues all alone at 16,17 years old.

Let's take Morgan for example. On her entrance interview, she exhibited the demeanor of a disengaged hippie who'd been through domestic violence and sexual abuse. These two ongoing tragedies in her life made her view love in a warped sense, which is why she's the poster child for a class like this. She's gifted. She's a creative. She's an artist. More importantly, she can bury and transform her hurtful experiences into witty stories, poems, and humor. Listen to her initial offering about her family and home life and see whether you can decipher what she really trying to say without saying it:

I remember one night I was watching TV while my father, Dave, was sleeping off one of his Mary Jane/Percocet highs and his pet python, Woody, sprung from his cage. I know Woody hadn't eaten in days and his rotund, slithering frame needed to be fed. While Woody slid across the room towards me I didn't think much of it because he was our pet snake. In fact, I remember feeling just as groggy and sleepy as Dave was but anyways. The last thing I remember seeing on television was "Love and Hip-Hop Hollywood" as I laid on Dave's lap.

Evidently, Woody made his way across the room measuring my little ten-year-old frame to feed his hunger. So, this huge ass snake started to wrap his strong frame around my little feet to my ankles, then my ankles up my legs, from my legs to my thighs. By then, I guess I could feel the squeeze and I woke up screaming "Dave! Dave! Dave! Woody is squeezing me too tight. Woody stop. Stop Woody. Dave! Dave! Please stop him."

I beat on her Dave's thigh, slapped his chest, trying to reach to see his face still he was so friggin high and Woody was so aggressive I just felt abandoned and scared. All in all, Dave didn't protect me; my father was in the room and couldn't protect me from this huge snake attacking me.

I started to like to get lightheaded from being in so much pain and realizing Dave wouldn't save me. Well, just then my mother walked in the door fusing because Dave hadn't answered his phone. She saw the situation I was in and threw some live treats for Woody to snack, so he pulled away from me and went to satisfy his hunger elsewhere.

As me and my mother left the living room, I looked back at Dave from over my mother's right shoulder. Although I was still a young preteen, I learned a valuable lesson that day: "A man can't save you, and don't expect them too!"

Now, when I asked this poor girl where the snake was currently, her reply was " oh, with Dave — he doesn't go anywhere without that damn snake".

Then, there's Morgan's best friend Danielle (Dani for short). The two of them are so different but so knitted together; opposites really do attract as it related to them. As Morgan is the grungy, love-hating, dissatisfied hippie adorned in black and gray every day, Dani is her innocent, naive, yet seductive southern belle who wears tightly fitted clothes with bold colors. Morgan doesn't believe in anyone while Dani believes in everyone, specifically the love of a man being the greatest of all things to her. Here's a lil' peep into her background from her entrance interview...

Grandma, I thought you said my daddy was coming to get me today?" Dani asked.

"I thought so too, baby, but something must've come up," her grandmother replied.

"My daddy's a damn liar, just like my mama said."

"Now wait a minute, lil' girl. You watch your DAMN mouth in this house. Besides, your mama ain't got much room to talk herself," her grandmother responded in her son's defense.

"But Nana, he said he was coming to get me!," Dani pleaded.

"And he still might be coming, Danielle. Just trust that he might make it. But one thing we do know is, ya damn mama won't be coming for you anytime soon. Always out chasing men from state to state like she's in heat," her grandmother mumbled under her breath.

Dani's lil' body went limp. She slumped to the floor, Indian style at her grandmother's feet. Every few seconds, she wiped away tears from under her nerdy glasses.

Her grandmother had to hide her disgust and anger for her absentee son. She couldn't say what she wanted out loud for her granddaughter was suffering enough, so she picked up her cell phone and text Dani's father immediately.

Her grandmother: Do you know what I'm looking at right now, son?

Dani's father: Huh? What do ya mean mama?

Her Grandmother: Your broken-hearted daughter. Do you know why she's heartbroken right now for the third weekend this month?

Dani's father: I am with my wife and kids right now, Mama. You know Adrienne ain't trying to let her come over here with our kids.

Her grandmother: So ... it's up to you to figure that part out. One thing I will promise you right now though, I have kept her in love with you thus far, let this happen one more time, and I promise you, I'll make her hate your guts forever.

Dani's father: Okay Ma. Should I call her or something?

Her grandmother: Nope. I got her today. You figure out how to prevent this happening again! See you in two weeks, son.

Her grandmother put her phone back down on the coffee table, and started to stare at her grandchild., "Look at me, baby!"

"No, Nana! I'm sad," Dani responded.

"Baby look at Nana now," she said again.

All her life, every time things got rough and Dani's emotions got the best of her, her grandmother knew how to stare her down until a big smile would cover her lil' brown-round face.

She picked Dani up off the floor, making her stand up before her. For about thirty seconds, it was a vicious stare down. Slowly, Dani's sadness started to break. Soon, she could no longer resist her Nana's eyes, and a big smile flashed across her face. As one last tear fell from her eyes, her grandmother wiped the tear away and said, "Guess what?

"What?" Dani asked, still trying to play sad.

"I'm about to make your favorite cake, baby. I know you wanna rub the sides of the cake pan and lick the batter off the spatula when I'm done, huh?"

Thirty minutes later, a happy and content Dani sat at the kitchen table propped up on pillows enjoying the remaining cake batter. "Nana, how much longer before the cake's ready 'cuz it smells so good. Mmm Mmm Mmm!"

Next, there's Chase. Chase is just what her names implies. She's a talented and a gifted writer, but she's too caught up in chasing the fake, artificial things in love and life. Image and her likes on social media networks are everything to her. She gets tons of on-line and in-person love. Great, right? Nope. Her obsession with other's approval displayed the results of extremely low self-esteem caused by outside factors. Her entrance interview was probably the most disturbing to me because I failed to experience hatred at such an early age ...

{Love and Basketball plays on her big screen television)

All's fair in love and basketball, right?" Omar Epps said angrily.

Just as Sanaa Lathan turned to walk away from the love of her life, the mood lightened and he belted out, "Hey! How about double or nothing?!"

Sanaa Lathan turned quickly and smiled realizing what that meant. They embraced passionately, solidifying the rekindling of their former love.

Chase whimpered. She heard footsteps approaching. She wiped away her tears, just as her mother burst in the closed door and caught her sobbing again.

"Oh my God! You must be watching another one of those tear-jerking, sappy love stories, huh Lil' Darky?" her mom suggested.

"Ma don't do that. This is real love. This is what real love looks like and feels like, and one day I'll find a love like Que and Monica from 'Love and Basketball' too," Chase intimated.

"Baby, you do realize that's just a movie right?" Her mom said nastily, taking another sip from her cup.

"Just because you don't believe in love, Ma, doesn't mean I shouldn't?" Chase expressed.

"Hey! I'm just trying to save you the heartache," her mom said slamming the door behind her.

She pushed the door back open suddenly and told her only child, "And what makes you think someone is going to love you looking like you look, with your ugly black self?" Her mom slammed the door shut again.

*Unscathed, Chase stared at the back of the door, and whispered "Such a cowardice b****!"*

*Chase didn't know what cowardice b**** really meant, but she'd seen it in a movie once, plus, it seemed to fit her real life now.*

Seconds later, her mother yelled back, "Your mother's a bitch, Darky! I know what you're saying about me back there. Sheesh! I useta say the same things about my mother with her drunk ass self," her mother added.

A clueless look covered Chase's face immediately.

"Really? I guess she's too drunk to realize she's talking about herself, stupid ass!" Chase whispered.

"Oh well!", as she picked up her remote, took a deep breath, and smiled again at the happy ending of "Love and Basketball."

"Let's see what's coming on next," she thought, "Ooh yes! 'Poetic Justice!'"

Then, there is Quincy and Dion who joined the class just to "get" to these high classed, easily stimulated ladies in my class. I did their entrance interviews together because they had an idea for a group project at the end of the course. When I asked them to tell me about love and life this was their response ...

Van Damme!!! Why is trying to love - like the most grizzly thing a man can do?" an exhausted Dion said to his best dawg. "I mean trying to just love a woman, nah damn that, just trying to get along with any female is like a pitbull fight. She doesn't care if your heart gets ripped to shreds or you get mangled to death emotionally trying to get with her.”

Dion continued in a confused tone, “Ain’t no love in the room when we’re standing around watching them pits get it in. Ain’t no love in the hearts of the owners that brought their dogs to fight. Nah, Sun. Everyone wants to witness the destruction.”

“Ugh! Go ‘head – Say more, I can tell you’re not finished yet,” Quincy said chuckling at his friend.

“Nah, seriously Que, loving a woman is like that energy between the two pits when they smash their faces together before the fight actually begins,” he paused, “You remember how it feels to be a part of that. That anticipation. That fear. That pride in the air. Feel me?”

“Gee, I don’t know what in the world you’re talking about?” Que responded, “but gon ‘head and get your negro logic on. I’m listening. What do they say in court though, point of order --umm Dion, you don’t even trust these Shebas in the first place?”

“Aye Que obviously, you don’t either,” Dion responded sarcastically, “because you stay getting played by these saltwater fish-es. Ha-ha!”

“Yeah whatever!” Que responded, “I holler at mine before go home every night, yaheard?”

“But do you love yours though? I mean in a real sense, Que. Are you in love or did you settle?” Dion inquired seriously, “Or, are you still stuck on the one who got away? Morgan!”

Dion continued, “Anyways, hear my flow though, think about those pitbull fights again. Think about how vicious the dawgs are *too each other?"*

Que said, "Of course, they're vicious. They're killers, and they're trained like that."

*"And that's what the f*** I'm talking about," Dion shouted.*

"These Shebas are trained by each other to be vicious and heartless like those pits. "Seriously, what would make a pit lock down on the neck of another dog while blood flies, bones crack, and muscles pop without any degree of sympathy?" Dion continued.

"Because they've been trained that way, D!" Que shouted back and then paused quickly.

"Oh ... Oh, wait," Que said smiling, "I got you now. You're saying the energy in the room is hardcore. Violent. Mmmmhmmmm. Vicious. Filled with those who have death on their minds."

"Exactly," Dion agreed, "Love is a game of players trained to kill, to build up their reputations as killers then receive the official stamp as a killer. So, when we find a nega living that life what do we say, 'that nega killin these hoes."

*"Well, love ain't s***, for real, for real. That's how I feel right now," Que shot back shaking his head.*

SO ... five souls, six including myself, trapped behind the doors of a classroom seeking to express ourselves in one way or another. May our art chase away the drama, or in our case, bring it closer to all of us.

" ... then leave us stranded?"

(Miss Bey's cell phone chimes)

"Excuse me class, I have to take this call!" she said. "Danielle! No, Chase, write down the names of everyone who shows their natural black 'you-know-what's' when I walk out of the door, please?"

"Why'd you ask her instead of me?" Dani said.

"Because you're always trying to be the boss of somebody!" Quincy said sarcastically.

"Why don't you shut up?" Dani said.

"No! ALL OF YOU SHUT UP," said Miss Bey, "Chase, do as I ask you, babygirl?"

"Yes Miss Bey," Chase said.

"Oh, and Dani you do always try to run everybody!" Miss Bey said with a sly smirk as she closed the door behind her.

(Everyone laughing hysterically at Dani)

"Ha-ha!" Morgan chuckled - just a chuckle though.

"Whoa! I don't care about the rest of them laughing -- but you Morgan?" Dani said acting all surprised.

Chase said, "Dani keep your voice down. That's my first

warning."

Thompson said, "Ain't no need of you looking evil lil' hoe. Stop being so damn mean."

"How about you..." Dani said whipping her head around until she saw who was talking to her.

"Mmmmhmmmm!" Morgan mumbled.

"Mmmmhmmmm, what?" Dani said, With your green-eyed ass."

Morgan said, "See, how stop and get all dumb for these stank boys?"

"Don't she though?" Chase said seconding the motion.

"Say what! What are you trying to say Chase? So, you are cosigning with this Yella' biscuit too, huh?"

"What I am saying is, be quiet for last time, lil' chocolate chip before I write that ass up!" Chase said emphatically.

(The Door Opens quickly)

Miss Bey returned visibly shook with tears streaming down her face.

"Oh, My Gawd! What's wrong Miss Bey?" Chase said.

"Babies," Miss Bey said subdued with heavy emotions, "Both of my parents have been in a terrible car accident. I gotta leave right now. You all head down to Miss Johnson's after-school class."

"Van Damme, I can't stand Miss Johnson, but..." said Thompson.

"Take yall asses down there - now," Miss Bey said emphatically and darted out the door once again.

(No one moved. One Minute. Two Minutes. Five minutes.)

"So - yall ain't going huh?" Dani said.

"Hell Nah!" Quincy said.

Dani, ever the goody-two-shoes, said, "Well I'm going and I'm telling on all you, bastards!"

Immediately Thompson said, "Dani, don't do that to us boo, come on back and chill with me. We can play with these computer games for the next two hours.

Dani settled down immediately and sat next to Thompson.

Morgan went off, "You're such a sucker for love a** biscuit!"

"Ain't she?" Chase said under her breath, "On the real, I hope Miss Bey's parents are okay?"

"Yeah?" Quincy said.

"Mane, why y'all even care?" Morgan said, "Most parents ain't worth a good hawk-n-spit anyway. I do have love for my auntie though ."

"You're just saying that because of what happened Saturday, Morgan," Dani said.

Quincy said, "Ohhhh, wait, what happened?"

Dani said, "One of yall - kind of like - got her in big trouble with Dave."

Quincy said, "What'd he do to his babygirl? Sic his snake on you?"

Morgan, usually the quick responder, said nothing.

Dani realized the hurt in her best friend's eyes and said, "Morg, what's wrong? I was just playing girl. Walk with me to the bathroom, please."

Morgan looked outside the window shielding her face from her classmates and said, "Nah, I'm good, mane."

Chase, the ever nosy one, said, "Morgan, you're right. Some parents ain't worth a penny, but still we should respect them."

"Whatever!" Thompson said, "What good is it for them to get us here and then leave us stranded? Parents are like, like, like selfish - kids for real."

"Truth!" said Chase, "sad, but true.".

Right on cue, Morgan said, "It may sound cruel, but it's real."

Chiming in, Dani said, "I don't know when the last time was I saw my trifling' dad?".

(most agreed)

"I know the last time I saw Dani's perfect applebum though," Thompson said while winking at Morgan at the same time.

"Oh! That was disrespectful!," Dani said, punching him in the chest playfully.

"Mmm Mmm Mmm!" said Chase, "Just like Morgan said, 'you're such a sucker for love,' Dani."

"... understand the laws of attraction ..."

"Mane, that was an hour of my life that I can't get back!" Morgan said in a depressed state.

"Right!" said Dani, "I feel so bad for Miss Bey. Having to bury both of your parents all by yourself."

"And where was the rest of her family? No one should have to go through that alone!" Chase said desperately, "It was like that scene from Cooley High at Cochise funeral. So sad."

"She didn't even have a man or boyfriend by her side? I mean nobody there," Morgan said, "I don't care about these Random dudes, but at least be there for me when I need support."

"Wait now! I've known Esther Bey for years, Niecy. She had many men standing around that funeral plot today. They just all know about each other," said Morgan's Aunt Ivey sarcastically.

"What'd you say Miss Ivey?" Chase said in disbelief, "Many men? As much as she tells us to forget about Randoms and get our money after high school?!"

"Listen, lil' girls! No women that looks like HER will ever walk these streets alone, doyouhearme?" Ivey said with a hearty laugh.

"Well now!" Dani said in her holier-than-thou tone, "I always thought so much more of Miss Bey than to have a trail of men following behind her."

"Dani - Chase - Morgan, you should know already, y'all have to understand the laws of attraction," Ivey said, sharing wisdom. "It's not about what you THINK is right, but what FEELS right as it relates to a man and a woman. She has to play with the cards the relationship gods have dealt her."

"Mane, y'all stop acting brand new," Morgan said cutting her auntie off. "Y'all now Miss Bey has all the teachers and students at the school in love with her now!"

"Well — since you put it like that — let's hurry back to the church for the repast because I'm hungry and I want to see if all of Miss Bey's hoes are going to show up to comfort her," Chase said with an evil grin.

———

(The four of them stroll into the fellowship hall)

"Chase!" a voice sounded from across the room.

Totally caught off guard, "Umm yes, Principal Marshall, I didn't expect to see you here?"

The Principal said, "Esther Bey is one of my best teachers and more than that, a close dear friend."

"Oh, I've heard how close," Chase said mumbling under her breath.

"What's that Chase?" he asked.

"Oh nothing! I'm starving and it's food in the atmosphere

so - see ya later?"

"So, why did I call you over here, right?" he said thinking Chase had a reason to hide from him.

"Hmm - you wanted to talk about the latest edition of the Monument High newsletter we released on-line on Thursday - perhaps?" Chase said hesitantly.

Principal Marshall said, "Exactly! I want to talk about who had the unmitigated gall to release an issue with the heading, *Sex, Love, and Hidden Cameras: A Monumental Scandal!*"

Chase dropped her head and said, "In lieu of great movies like *All the President's Men* where journalists are protected from revealing sources or shying away from the truth, I'd like to say as the acting Editor-in-Chief that is my responsibility ultimately."

"Well, Miss Editor-in-Chief find your way to my office first thing Monday morning because your journalistic confessions and claims and have embarrassed some of the students and a lot of the teachers at our fine school," he assured her.

Chase said, "I'll be there Mr. Marshall, but I hope you're not expecting me to apologize for anything. We've had more than a 1000 downloads and 1000 more visitors to our page since it was released less than 48 hours ago, so okay!"

"Take it how you want to young lady," Principal Marshall said, "I'm still the supreme authority at this school."

—

"Oh, my Gawd!" Dani said stopping in her tracks.

"Mane, what now?" Morgan asked.

The only table with seats available is..." Dani said before Morgan cut her off.

"... Over there by Thompson with his big goofy self," Morgan said with disdain. "Every time you see him or get near him you start acting simple. Let's go. Come on Auntie."

(They reach the table)

"What's up Morgan? Danielle? Now, who is this lovely young lady here?" Thompson asked about Aunt Ivey.

"Lawd Hammercy! I'm Ivey, Morgan's aunt," Ivey said replying craftily, "Who are you, mister?"

"Mane, that ain't nobody, but big clumsy Thompson," Morgan interjected, "He thinks he's the next Lebron James or something, but don't let him fool ya."

"Oh my, Mr. Tall and Basketball! Are those your real eyes, young man?" Ivey asked about his hazel eyes.

"Yassssssssssss child," Dani said as thirsty as she could be. Morgan shot her a quick glance as if to say, 'have some respect for yourself'.

Thompson cleared his throat, "Sad, sad occasion we have here. I hate to see my boo thang Miss Bey in so much pain."

"It is very sad, isn't it, Mr. Hazel?" Ivey said. "I didn't expect to see any young male students here being that y'all usually shy away from two things: funerals and weddings. And, speaking of weddings ain't that Senior over there with his new boo?"

"Auntie, don't start? This ain't the time nor place," said Morgan.

"The time or place for what exactly?" Chase said sitting her plate down on the table.

"Nothing!" Dani said smiling at Aunt Ivey. "So umm, Thompson, the prom is coming up real soon."

Stag!!!" Thompson said sharply and loud enough to disturb everyone within ten feet of their table.

"Well!" said Dani.

"But, if I do take somebody, then..." said Thompson staring in Morgan's direction.

"Stag!" Morgan said right back in his direction while winking her eye at Dani, "I'm not a prom person."

Suddenly, Morgan's phone rings loudly causing her to jump up from the table and scurry off quickly. "Girl, who has you running to take a phone calls outside in the middle of your favorite teacher's funeral," Ivey said boldly as Morgan scampered across the floor of the dining hall.

———

(Across the room Miss Bey meets the Officiant)

"Sister Bey, the first lady apologizes for not being able to come but she sent her heartfelt condolences," said Pastor Thomas.

"Pastor, you don't know how incredible you've been to me in the past week or so. There's absolutely no way I could have made it without you and your church family. Funny...I wish I could take you all with me into tomorrow?" said Miss Bey with a sad confused look.

She continued, "How does a person go on after this?"

Pastor Thomas reached in his back pocket and grabbed his wallet and handed her a business card.

"Here's our card with the church's phone number on it," he said while pulling out his cell phone, "give me your cell number please."

Esther gave him her cell phone number along with a huge hug and a kiss on the jaw. A move that obviously made more than a few eyebrows raise, male and female. Cleverly, instead of dealing with her hoes aka her male entourage, she sent the funeral home guys on their way and caught a ride back to her house with Pastor Thomas.

CHAPTER 5

"... I'm ready for whatever ..."

It's Monday morning. Chase and her staff are posted up outside of Principal Marshall's office for the big showdown. Chase was smart enough to surround herself with other good writers who also loved being nosey, messy, and followers of the crowd. Call it destiny or good management that her bestie was the assistant editor and bae was the main reporter. After Chase told them of her encounter with the principal, they sought to get out in front of the situation. So, first thing Saturday morning they posted a blog entitled, "Monument High Newspaper Staff Threatened for Speaking Truth!"

Students in the know offered encouragement and support as they sat and waited on their "judge". Still, the three of them knew it could be a high cost for outing so much truth in a school newspaper, especially one that broadcasts over the internet before hard copies are printed.

"I mean what's the worst thing that could happen to us?" Tremaine asked. "We didn't do diddly but tell the truth for real, for real."

"At this point, I'm ready for whatever," Monique said like a lioness protecting her cubs. "If old man Marshall wasn't ..."

"If old man Marshall wasn't what?" Principal Marshall said walking out his office quickly. They had no idea he was there because the door was locked, and the lights were off. Moreover, he had heard all their plans on how to deal with him about this situation.

"Come on in," the principal said as he turned on the lights and beckoned them to have a seat. "No need to look shook now. I mean, what's the worst thing that can happen? Other than your words preventing you from graduating this coming June."

"Huh?" Chase said looking him up and down in disbelief and disgust,

"No, I'll see you one at a time. Chase you are first because ultimately you had to make the final call," he said.

As the door closed, the reality of the situation set in for Monique and Tremaine.

"Oh, he's trying to go at our necks, ain't he?" Tremaine said visibly vexed.

"Ha-ha, yes! And the one person who could smooth this over easily won't be back for a while now," Monique said referring to the senior advisor of the newspaper.

"You're joking right? Miss Bey was our ace in the hole!" Tremaine said.

"Yeah she was, but ..." Monique said, "we gotta fend for ourselves this time. Damn these hidden cameras and secret investigations."

Both laughed nervously, wondering what the future would hold. Holding up one fist in the air like a Black man protesting the 1968 Olympics, Tremaine said, "Be strong, Chase. Hold fast my sister!"

Shaking her head, Monique said, "see that's the kind of foolishness that's got us here in the first place."

—

"Good Morning Biscuit!" Dani said.

"Morning my ass," Morgan said crawling in Dani's Tahoe.

"Oh, that's how you're feeling this morning bestie after I've come all the way across town for your high-yella green-eyed ass? See the next time you roll with me to school!" Dani said emphatically.

"Dani, I told you–wait, excuse me–I *asked* you to come early because I need to do something before school." Morgan said.

"I heard you and WHAT? If you hadn't taken so much time sharing another one of your crazy, suicidal dreams with me then I would have been here 20 minutes earlier," said Dani, "Plus, you never TOLD me what you needed or wanted to do anyways."

"Take me by Quincy's house right fast, mane," She said, "I need to grab something from him for school."

"Something like what?" Dani said.

"Something like none of your damn business, mane!" said Morgan, "You're really feeling yourself this morning huh?"

"Nope. Just protecting my friend because I don't like or

trust Quincy! And, you know that" Dani said.

"You are funny acting mane!" Morgan said, "But you trust Thompson fully, huh?"

Morgan's phone rings. She answers it on the first ring causing Dani to do a double take, remembering the mysterious phone call at the funeral.

"Hel–Hel–Hello! Hey Hey!" Morgan answers apprehensively.

Dani faintly hears a guy screaming at Morgan.

"I'm on my way. We're right around the corner. I promise!" Morgan said nervously.

Dani asked, "Who are you talking to? And why are they talking to you like that?"

Morgan quieted Dani. "I said I am right around the corner!" Morgan said again.

There's more yelling through the phone. Dani could hear the guy asking if she could handle the job or not.

"This will never happen again. That's a promise. I need this too badly, mane!" Morgan assured the guy. As they pull up in front of the apartment complex, Morgan told the guy, "Open the door please. I'm on my way right now."

Five minutes later, Morgan dashed back to the truck and hopped in sounding jovial suddenly. "Hey mane! I really appreciate the ride this morning. We don't have time for breakfast, but I'll fill your tank up and take us to Chipotle after school, okay?"

Dani looked genuinely concerned, but there's only one thing she loves more than tall, dark skinned guys, and that is money. She responded, "Okay girl! That's cool. I guess I'm not supposed to ask who the hell that was yelling at you like that a little while ago, huh? Biscuit, please don't tell me that was Quincy talking to you like that?"

"Nah, nah!" Morgan said, "It was this guy at his apartment who was using his phone. That's all."

"... sworn me to secrecy ..."

The minister announced to the congregation, "I now pronounce you husband and wife. You may salute your bride! May the congregation please stand, and for the first time, I'd like to introduce Mr. James Sr. and LaTonya Smith."

—

"Congratulations, LaTonya, girl!" Ivey said, offering her the fakest hug while wearing the shadiest smile. "Hey listen! You better take good, good care of my dear friend now!"

The newly anointed bride responded, "Mmm! I know y'all go way, way back, Miss Ivey, and I am very, very, very thankful you've brought him up through the years, but I promise you, I got it from here."

Staring from the background and watching this awkward exchange take place was James Sr., his heart pounding a million times a minute. Senior, a locally renown "maintenance man," had been "slow-roasting" with Ivey on and off for the past 20 years or so.

"Hey Ivey!! Hey Morgan!" I'm glad y'all made it," said Senior nervously as Ivey made her way towards him.

"Ummm hmm! I am so, so sure, Senior. Well, congratulations to you both, yaknow? May y'all find marital bliss and heaven on earth with one another," Ivey declared, like a woman happily handing over her leftovers to a newbie. Yet, before Ivey sashayed away, she leaned in as if to kiss Senior's cheek and whispered something in his ear that made his eyes bug out twice their normal size.

When they got in the car, Morgan, who always loved the ratchet dramatic shenanigans, wasted no time in asking her Auntie, "What did you whisper in Senior's ear because his eyes looked like he'd seen a ghost, mane?"

"Babygirl, I promise you, what I said to that nervous and shivering man, is too, too grown for your young ears, yagotme?" Ivey assured her niece with a chuckle.

"Really Auntie? I don't see why not. You know how many times you've sworn to me secrecy in the past 15 years," Morgan laughed, "Some stories I desperately wanted to hear, others I wish I could erase from my damn memory. But later for all that mane, spill it -- now please?!"

Ivey smirked at her young protege, knowing her sister, Morgan's mother, would kill her for opening her eyes to the games she played and ran on simple minded men.

Morgan kept asking repeatedly like her brain would be stuck forever if she couldn't get the latest, juicy gossip from her fav auntie.

"See, I know that look. You want to tell me because you're messy like that. I know y'all already. I know y'all history. I know how you really feel about Senior. I also know you are a master at playing these men in these types of situations — so please share what in the hell you whispered in his ear?"

"Watch your damn mouth, Morgan. That's one too many now," a smiling Ivey checked her sassy niece. "I'm going to tell ya mammy you are being a nasty mouthed little heifer!"

"Anyways. What did you ask me again?" Ivey said, hoping to throw her off the scent.

"Ugh! Auntie, would you please stop playing with me. What did you say to that man?" pleaded Morgan.

"Oh, oh yeah, that was your question!" Ivey giggled.

"Well," Ivey paused.

"WELL!" Morgan shouted.

"I told him that I hope LaTonya has a good swimming pool because he won't be diving in mine anymore," Ivey admitted as a shady, sinister smile slid across her face.

"Auntie!" Morgan yelled, "I know you did not tell Senior that inside of the church, in front of his new bride, AND on their wedding day, mane. No!"

"Indeed, I did, Sugar Plum," Ivey responded, "And I meant every word! I only do married men if they were married when we met."

CHAPTER 7

"... Keep it 100 ..."

"What happened to you?" said a worried and aggravated Monique. "We waited outside for you until security made us go to class."

"Principal Marshall is trying to do me wrong, 'Nique. He's not a little mad, he's big mad girl. He said our quote-unquote 'allegations' in the school paper were divisive and evil," Chase said. "Now little does he know we have witnesses, dates, and stories from the actual people on this one, but yeah anyway."

"But you know what I'm finding out Chase, he's nervous—like shook for real. Everyone wants him fired: students, teachers, staff, even the lunch ladies," Monique said with a chuckle. "But that doesn't excuse him from trying to set you up and it doesn't mean you can just freaking disappear on us when we're in this together."

"I didn't disappear—well I kind of did," Chase said. "Mr. Buchanan was leaving school and he saw me —well — saw me umm — disturbed..."

"He saw you crying in other words, keep it 100!" Monique said.

Chase replied, "Anyways—so we sat outside the school and talked till he brought me home. I couldn't concentrate in class after seeing Principal Marshall for two straight hours.”

“Excuse me,” Monique said dumbfounded.

“Yes, Nique, this dude doesn’t want me to graduate!” Chase said sadly.

“Wait! Mr. Buchanan drove you home. Hmmm okay. First, Mr. Marshall is a dumb-stupid. Second, that’s a lawsuit waiting to happen. You’re an honor roll student, Chase, so—how does he stop you from graduating for some online newspaper? How does that work?” Monique said.

“See, that’s the same thing, John, umm Mr. Buchanan said...” Chase replied.

“John?” said a puzzled Monique.

“Listen, not now okay?” Chase said, cutting her off quickly. “I’m just saying John swore me to secrecy on the Principal Marshall thing. And, that I should just hold on and keep my grades up and ... ?”

“And what?” Monique said.

“And quit the paper. He suggested I step down as editor in chief and let you and Tremaine take over. Said y’all have to throw me under the bus sort of speak,” Chase replied.

“Clearly, clearly, that’s not happening,” Monique said in aggressively. “You’re my dawg. I ain’t turning my back on you, Chase. We did this together.”

“Listen lil’ girl, John said — well Mr. Buchanan said — whoever said — that could free us up altogether because as of right damn now Principal Marshall is ready to have a full blown trial with those involved in our allegations with all of Monument high serving as witnesses."

"Damn!!!!!!!" Monique said.

"'Nique, listen — things just got real!" Chase said emphatically.

(Both of them sat there a few moments in utter disbelief)

CHAPTER 8

"Oh, my Gawd! Thompson is heading over here," Dani screamed to Morgan under her breath.

"Mane, you've seen how real my life has been this morning, do you really think I give a flying fudge about Thompson the-the —big basketball blooper guy? No!" Morgan replied.

When it comes to men, Dani believed that getting a man was like #LifeGoals; the harder she worked to get him, then the sooner she could have him in her clutches ... forever. Morgan, on the other hand, absolutely hated how Dani carried herself around available men.

"Danielle!" Morgan ranted.

"Uh oh! It must be serious if you're calling out my government name?" Dani responded.

"Whatever, mane! When it comes to these ninjas, why do you always put all your chips on the table at the beginning of the game? A woman should save her best plays for different stages of the game," Morgan insisted, "but do what you do though."

"No, don't say that Morgan. I want your help," Dani followed, "but I, and I repeat, I do not want to play no cotdamn games with little boys. I just don't have time for the games and the lies."

"Okay heifer, but you do have time to keep getting your heart broken though, aye? When are you going to learn love don't love nobody?" Morgan chided. "And Love owes you nothing but the game of it all? Besides, the juiciest most intense love stories are those where the woman is being pursued, and her and the perfect guy keep missing opportunities to fall in love with each other. It's all cat and mouse—aka it's A Game."

"You're one to talk. You freaking hate love, Morgan," Dani said sarcastically.

"Damn right; it's all fake. In fact, love ain't worth the four letters it takes to spell it," Morgan responded.

"So, you can tell me how to catch a man, but not how to love one though, hoe? You are such a hoe!" Dani said laughing.

"Exactly!" Morgan stated.

"Forget that!!! I expect these negas to treat me royally and cater to all my needs. Hell, I ain't the average chick. This body and kitty is oh so official," Dani bragged.

"You are official huh, Dani? Yeah, officially, alone!" Morgan scoffed playfully.

"Damn you Morgan, you tell these negas to eff off and be gone and their only comeback is 'but I can't Morg, you're special baby'. What the hell is that? I give my all, workout, and some more and you barely lift a finger for a man, yet you keep them all wrapped around your finger. How?" asked Dani emphatically.

"I don't know, hell! I don't know, mane," answered Morgan.

"I will admit though it doesn't make sense. You chase them, they run away. I run away and they chase me," Morgan continued shrugging her shoulders.

"... a bite, a bottle, and go chill ..."

Loving you is easy 'cause you're beautiful – making love with you is all I wanna do.

Loving you is more than just a dream come true – and everything that I do is out of loving you.

(Plays through Chase's headphones)

She sings to herself, "la la la la la, la la la la la, la la la la la la la la la la... do do do doo ohhhhhhhh!"

Her cell phone bling lights up, cutting off her music momentarily.

"Chase!!!" Monique screamed, "Heifer, have you heard?"

"Heard what, Nique?" Said Chase.

"What in the—GIRL, where have you been, under a rock?" Monique said excitedly.

"I've been on my love songs for past couple days to calm down from the stress," Chase said.

"Chase, get online NOW,' Monique said shouting, "Log in to the school's website ASAP!"

"Ugh! This better be good because Minnie Rippleton was singing to my soul," Chase said, scrambling through her phone.

"Oh, My Gawd!" Chase screamed.

"Yeah Heifer. Yeah," Monique said.

"Nique, is this a joke? Too much is going on for the games. She said anxiously.

"Chase, it's ALL REAL," Monique said in affirmation, "He's gone for real."

"What?" Chase said reading the news brief out loud, "Principal Daniel Marshall steps down as head of Monument high amongst allegations that he and several members of the faculty were engaged in wrongful and incriminating actions."

"Yes Girl!" Monique said cheering along to the article, "We be free, Boo-boo."

"Oh, My Gawd! Thank you Nique," said Chase. "You know he told me everything was going to be alright."

"Who?!" Monique said.

"Let me call you right back girl. I must call my baby right now. It's real important," Chase said.

Monique replied, "Wait --What? Tremaine is right --"

(Click -- Phone hangs up immediately)

Tremaine said, "So, what happened? What'd she say Nique?"

"She said she'll call me back," Monique said confused, "I think she's about to call you though."

"Call me?" Tremaine said. "I ain't heard from her all

day and that's my girl—well, supposed to be. Stuff has been different a few days."

"Always the overly excited one," Monique lightened the mood. "Aye it's whatever—my parents are gone for the weekend. Let's grab a bite, a bottle, and go chill at my house 'til Chase comes through."

"Cool," a puzzled Tremaine replied, "but, I ain't holding my breath 'til she gets here."

"... I don't play with my family ..."

For the most part, it's simple here in Monument. Simple like me walking barefoot on this damp, freshly cut grass with a honeysuckle in between my teeth. It's this ole wrap dress my granny useta wear without bra or panties. Right now, I'm broken. I'm grieving, but I'm freely expressing myself just because it feels good. Sometimes in life everyone must get back to when it was all so simple, and it feels major. ....Now, it's time to reclaim me, or some piece of the broken pieces me and live life like it's golden.

After my parents died suddenly — tragically, I spazzed out for a minute, remaining inside my house for weeks. I chose to stay on the family's estate hidden way back in the woods rather than moving away like the rest of my family had. My house became the perfect hideout for my Random sexcapades. I needed comfort without scrutiny or risking being seen by one my babies accidentally. Something had come over me after my parents were gone; a load was lifted, and I could finally be me rather than the sheltered daughter of the proud yet strict Moorish Grand Sheikh. I had come to my senses.

Coincidentally, every single man who'd ever crushed on me suddenly had a chance to fulfill his dreams. Of course, I hate myself for being such a hypocrite, especially since I teach my babies not to be this way. Still, here I am being this way and loving it. But hey, I'm in my mid-30s, no kids of my own, still fly as can be, and Shawty gotta build a life of her own.

Awfully, I tell my students to never let the emptiness they feel allow them to be made a spectacle of by some random individual. Someone told me once that this type of emotionless sex is just masturbation using another person's body rather than your hand or a toy. So, I did something so common, but it was gravely needed: I sought out the Reverend who officiated my folks' funeral. Looking back on it, I don't know if it was a good or bad idea.

Now, after weeks of close, emotionally stirring counseling sessions with him, Pastor Thomas and I have grown remarkably close. So close, I believe the First Lady is picking up on some of our chumminess. Like most preachers' wives, the First Lady feels the need to protect her husband from needy women. However, she has gracefully given me a pass because she says she couldn't imagine the deep hurt I've experienced from burying my parents alone.

Although I don't think she cares for our bond, I feel like she knows it would be petty to accuse a grieving woman like myself of being sneaky and sleezy with the pastor. Besides, I needed Love. I needed comfort. The First Lady needed assurance of her husband's faithfulness but for now, she's allowing me to play naive and granting me some leeway. I think my time is running out though after this past Sunday's encounter.

—

"Sister Esther," the first lady called as they headed toward their cars after a Sunday afternoon quartet service.

"Yes, First Lady!! How may I be of service?" Esther asked.

First Lady Joy responded, "I'm just inquiring how your soul is fairing after your loss. I must admit I have held you up in prayer and even asked the pastor about your spirit during the recent counseling sessions. I hope you don't take my asking as prying though?"

"Oh, is that right?" Esther murmured.

The First Lady continued, "The pastor is very strict about the privacy of his counseling sessions.

At that very moment, something sinister welled up in Esther when she perceived First Lady's insecurity about her present camaraderie with the pastor.

"Sister Joy let me say something real to you. You are married to a devout man who has rocked and cradled my wounded spirit through this entire situation. I am thankful that you let me borrow him twice a week to give me the encouragement that I need right now," said Esther. "You both have a wonderful Sunday evening now."

Esther's deceitful words disturbed the First lady, realizing Esther was taking full advantage of her present circumstance. Just then, Sister Joy, who grew up in the sinister streets of the Bayou too, moved awfully close to Esther until their wide brimmed hats began to touch.

"Look here, Yella Heifer, I don't play with my family, so I suggest you get yourself together and find your own man. And furthermore, someone else to handle your counseling sessions because you and Pastor ain't going anotha-furtha', Yaundeestandmeh?"

The First Lady continued, "What has it been—six or seven weeks now—yes, I think you can handle things on your own from now, hoe."

Esther quickly replied, "Whatever Thomas...I meant to say, Pastor Tommy, told me I could use his shoulder to cry on until I am I am FULLY recovered. Well, guess what? I ain't there yet!"

"Oh, is that right? We'll see about that Ms. Heifer. Oops! I meant to say, Miss Esther," the First Lady replied.

—

Boys and girls, it's on now. And soon First Lady Joy will see Esther Bey ain't no one to play with. I know, I know, I know, I'm playing with Fire. I also know that this makes me a hypocrite and the one things that my babies hate is a fake, partly because I've taught them to always respect themselves and never be ashamed of what or who they see in the mirror. I just hope when this season of my life is over that they won't smell this hoe spirit on me.

" ... and stop believing everything ..."

"Miss Bey!!!!! Oh, My Gawd!!" Dani said jumping up to hug and squeeze the neck of her favorite teacher. "Welcome back. I've missed you!"

"Where have you been?" Thompson asked.

"How have you been? What have you been up to?" Dani said hopping around her like a child.

"Nah, forget all that — WHO have you been up to?" said a sarcastic Morgan.

"Ugh Morgan. That's rude," Dani said with her mouth stretched wide in unbelief.

"Hush up Morgan!" Miss Bey said with a smirk. "And stop believing everything Ivey whispers in your lil' ears, okay?"

"Whatever!" Morgan jived back.

"Seriously Miss Bey, it's good to have you back. So much has happened since you've been gone," Chase said, shaking her head.

"Oh, is that right?" Miss Bey inquired. "So much huh — you've become Miss TMZ in the streets (aka the halls of MHS)."

Chase said, "I guess but... "

"You guess huh?" Miss Bey said, smiling. "I want to thank

y'all so much. It's been hard some days but thinking about y'all helped me to get through it all. Also, I really appreciate all of you who showed up for the homegoing/funeral services because your energy meant so, so much to me."

"Okay, okay. That's enough of the mushy stuff, mane," Morgan said. "We were trying to figure out which one of those tall fine black men was your thang boo, mane?"

"Really Morgan -- again," a shocked Dani said.

"It's only a month left before summer break, Miss Bey. Why'd you come back now anyway? You could have had a long summer vacay?" Chase asked her.

"Well, Chase," she responded, "it's the perfect time for me to return to watch my babies get fitted for their graduation caps and gowns."

"So — what's changed," Miss Bey asked, "other than —"

Morgan cut her off saying, "You missed do-gooder-Dani's entire three-day relationship with Thompson!"

"Random! Ha-Ha!" Chase yelled out humorously.

"Morgan!!!" Miss Bey shouted while making her way to Morgan's desk, "What is going on in that head of yours today?"

Morgan smiled back very fake before offering, "What, Miss Bey? I'm good, mane."

"And again, what did I tell you about ending every sentence with that 'mane' stuff?" Miss Bey said stooping down to whisper into Morgan's left ear, "Young lady, what in the hell happened to your face? Come outside with me — NOW"

(The room fell silent as Morgan is not the one to be called out by anyone).

"Morgan who put their hands on you. Is Dave back again?" Miss Bey said with conviction.

"No, no, no nothing like that mane. Everybody keeps fu--, I'm sorry keeps getting on my nerves," Morgan fired back.

"And! Is that well enough reason for someone to bruise your face up, huh — huh? Tell me Morgan? Is it?" Miss Bey asked.

"Me and Dani? We -- we had a fight last week?" Morgan admitted.

Miss Bey closed her eyes and shook her head. "Thompson, right?"

"It's not like that! Well, it wasn't supposed to go down like that," Morgan said sadly.

"So, was it Dani or Thompson that whooped your head like this? Come On spill it!" Miss Bey demanded again.

"Neither!" Morgan replied.

"Not Dave, thank God, not Thompson or Danielle, so ...?" Miss Bey paused for the answer.

"Mane, I'm gone," Morgan said, walking off.

"What about your cap and gown Morgan?" Miss Bey asked.

Morgan stopped, turned around slowly, inhaled-exhaled

deeply, and said, "Mane, I was just here waiting on Danielle so we could talk and hopefully she give me a ride home. To be honest, I'm not graduating Miss Bey."

"Stop it. I don't believe that," Miss Bey said.

"Look I have too much else going on right now and school is not a priority. Sorry Miss Bey," Morgan said walking swiftly down the hallway.

Miss Bey watched her walk down the entire hallway until she pushed heavily out of the double doors.

CHAPTER 11

They say time heals all wounds, not in Morgan's case. It could not erase the emotional and physical scars left from dealing with her abusive father and his pet snake. It almost served as a prelude to her dealings with this psycho fool, Quincy. Still, Morgan's attitude towards men remained unscathed.

"Mane, these Randoms serve no freaking purpose in my life — really on this earth, except when I feel like toying with them" she told Dani.

"They are just utilities .... like gas, electricity, heat, and air conditioning," Morgan added.

"Is that why you slept with my boyfriend?" Dani obviously hurt, "To prove some kind of sick point."

"Nope — mane — I slept with that Random Thompson because he got me high, and he had special instruments for a girl like me to play with. The End!" Morgan said coldly.

Dani chimed in, "Heifer, we are high school seniors, and you sound like your Auntie right now. It's like you're trying to bring in some new type of female that does for herself first, and only lean on a man when she wants to, never ever because she must. I'm sure my grandmother's doing flips in her grave hearing this foolishness. She always said you gotta let a man be a man while you remain a lady!"

"Damn that Dani. It's time to flip it mane and reverse things. I am the prototype: a real, official boss," she marveled her best friend with "game". "Not in a fake, commercialized, wonder-woman type of way. No!!! For real, for real, a woman must accept 'her' truth, her position, and walk in it, mane."

"Ummm!" Dani thought then responded carefully. "It's funny though your Auntie Ivey always said that you will never fully walk in your powers because you still don't realize how powerful you really are," dropping a bomb on Morgan's overwhelming ego.

"Oh, is that right?" Morgan said. "Ivey doesn't know me. I just act like I don't know what time it is mane! She thinks she sees something in me that I don't. I know this game, mane."

Dani said, "Well it seems you're losing the game to me because we are supposed to be graduating today but instead you're in here telling pimp stories with a swollen eye and bruised up arms. Really Morgan?"

—

A nervous Tremaine asked Monique, "What are you going to say to Chase?"

"I'm just not going to deal with it. I mean, I did speak with her briefly last night but," Monique said, stuttering.

"But what?" Tremaine said leaning in on Monique's partial responsibility in this situation.

"Hell!! You ARE her man, right? Check your lady, player!"

Monique added trying to insult his manhood.

"Shawty, that's supposed to be your best friend, so check yourself!" Tremaine jabbed back.

"Listen, I don't — I don't," Monique said looking at him softly.

Tremaine pulled her close and said, "Listen we're both wrong here, but it feels — it feels so right!"

A suddenly feverish Monique said, "Tremaine. I hate you for doing this to my friend, but she ..."

"But SHE - ain't here!" Tremaine said, taking full advantage of her moment of weakness.

As he spoke, Monique saw fire in his eyes. He snatched her by the elbow and shoved her back into the backseat of his mom's truck. He threw their caps on the front seat and preceded to make a mess of their freshly pressed gowns.

Ten minutes later, they're dashing towards the graduation line, both wearing looks of satisfaction mixed with guilt and revenge.

Meanwhile, Chase is holding their spots in line. They've ignored her phone calls and texts all day, but Monique's crafty mind springs into action. She decides to call Chase now while running holding her heels in one hand and the phone in the other.

"Chase, this dumb-dumb Tremaine hits a pothole and blows the tire out on the way here," Monique tells Chase on the fly.

"Really? So why didn't dumb-dumb just call an Uber," Chase screamed at Tremaine through the phone.

"My point exactly— where are you?" Monique asked.

"There she is," Tremaine spotted her across the room.

"Well, dumb-dumb you almost caused y'all to miss graduation, huh?" Chase said snarly.

"Listen, save it, Chase, I was busy trying to get us here!" Tremaine answered, "and where were you all day?"

"I was — where I was at — and?" Chase fired back.

"And nothing...well I could say the same thing," he said.

"No, you can't SAY the same thing because the same rules don't apply to you, buddy!" Chase said in a nasty tone.

"Anyways! Chase just be happy we made it — Damn," Monique said with an attitude.

"Okay, but I mean ..." Chase said, "why do y'all look like y'all robes just came out of the plastic package."

"We changed the tire -- remember dumb-dumb," Tremaine said to Chase aggressively.

"I guess you all didn't have enough sense to take your robe off first, huh?" Chase sensing something strange.

"Nope!" he boasted.

Chase cut her eye at Monique, "I guess you actually got out the vehicle to help change a tire, huh?"

"Yes!" Monique answered with a nasty tone.

"Umph! That's strange you don't even pump your own gas unless it's necessary," Chase said challenging Monique.

"Anyways, I hear *Pomp and Circumstance* playing so let's get to moving y'all," Monique redirects the discussion.

"Yes! Let us get to moving!" Chase said emphatically. "Because none of this Randomness is making sense."

CHAPTER 12

"Check myself before what ..."

Unbeknownst to himself, Pastor Thomas came home to a human tornado named Joy Thomas. Because he's totally exhausted after preaching twice for two services at different locations, there's only three things he wants right now: a hot meal, a hot bath, and a cool cozy bed. But Nah hell, none of that is in his near future nor anything remotely close to it.

(The Alarm chimed loudly)

"Hey, Hey first lady! It smells good in here. What are you hooking up for the Pastor-in-charge?" Pastor asked.

"Mmm ... Oh, I hear you're in charge, alright?" she scoffed.

"What?" He frowned, trying to decipher from that response whether she's pleased or pissed.

"What in the hell are you talking about, Joy? I'm tired now! I don't feel like it!" he continued.

Joy responded viciously, "Oh, I'm just Amen-ing what you said, baby. You said that you're the pastor in charge, right? Oh, oh, I am surprised I haven't heard just how in charge you are from your Esther lately!"

"Esther who?" he asked, "Are you talking about lil' Esther Bey? Now, what does that supposed to mean?"

Joy spazzed, "First of all Nega, I know you keep your counseling sessions secret from anyone outside the room, but ummm...I asked lil' Esther how she was doing today and..."

"Wait! What?" Thomas interrupted her immediately. "Why would you do that? You know how I feel about that. This is my friggin' career we're talking about here. People entrust their biggest secrets with me, knowing that it won't go anywhere else."

"Well what-the-hell-ever, I just had to," Joy replied, wearing a look of embarrassment.

"Never mind that though," she quickly switched the subject. Why did this heifer start staring in the distance with her eyes twinkling talking about how wise you are, and how lucky I am to have a man like you, and how you said you'd have her back until she fully got over her grief. Ummm answer that pastor?" She continued.

"So, you mean to tell me that you seriously have a problem with that, Joy?" he paused for a long minute rubbing the back of his head. "Damn! You are acting real friggin' petty right now."

"Do you really think I give a damn how you think I'm making you feel right now? Really nega? I could care less BUT I want it to stop right now, Thomas!" she said sternly. "Oh, and she called you by your first name instead of pastor too, nega! I wonder why?" She finished.

"Oh girl, please!" he shouted, "this couldn't have waited

until tomorrow morning. You know what kind of day I've had."
"Hell no, I don't want this heifer using your anointing and devotion to your work to-to -to-to manipulate because ..."

"Shut up, Joy!" Thomas shouted. "I haven't a clue as to where all this is coming from."

"Nah, Nah. I can't do that, and I won't do it," Joy screamed.

Thomas responded, "But you best to check yourself, Joy before ..."

Joy quickly cut him off, "Check myself before what? What nega, because you ain't going to do nothing but cancel them sessions ... now!"

"Huh! I be damned!" he finished the conversation, slamming the bathroom door behind him.

CHAPTER 13

"A predator must hunt. Its prey must tease to make the predator want them ..."

"Shush! Shush! Quiet babygirl!" Dave told his 7-year-old at the time.

"Watch how Woody waits and waits and waits almost like he's dead, camouflaging himself along the walls of the tank, like some shrubbery or something. His skin is his cover. His patience is his God," David continued.

"I'm scared for the mouse, Daddy," Morgan said.

"Quiet now. Watch the mouse move. It moves carefully, not being used to its new surroundings. But, because the snake waits like it does, the mouse doesn't perceive him to be what he is," David said, using his index finger to describe this moment.

"Why doesn't the snake just strike as soon as he sees his food moving, Daddy?" Morgan asked innocently. "It's like he's just playing with the mouse — like it's some sort of game or something."

"A predator must hunt. Its prey must tease to make the predator want them," her daddy answered.

A frowning Morgan then asked, "But it's sad, Daddy. He's about to die, and he doesn't even know it."

"Well Umm," David tried to make his point gently, "Morgan,

in my mind, I believe the mouse knows something. Something tells it that its time is about to end."

(And just as David spoke the Python struck and swallowed the mouse whole.)

"Oooh!!! Oooweee!!! He got 'em Daddy!" Morgan shouted while jumping in David's lap.

"Yes, he did, babygirl," David replied, "Yes he did!"

"Now, baby, look at me, you remember that little boys are just like that python, waiting for unsuspecting, naive lil' girls," he taught Morgan.

"Aw, daddy, you're silly," said a bashful Morgan.

"No, now I'm serious. Never be like that mouse who got put in a new environment and got ate up because it didn't know it was in a dangerous situation, okay?" David instructed her.

"So, Daddy, are all boys like Woody or just some of them?" She asked sincerely.

"Babygirl, when you see a snake on the ground, do you go the other way, or do you walk up and try to pet him?" David asked. Morgan answered, "I ain't going to put my hands on him because he might be poisonous!"

"Exactly!!!!!" Dave smirked, "Don't touch any boys because they all might be poisonous. Yaundeestandmeh?"

—

Just then, Morgan turns and smiles at Ramel.

"What's on your mind, green eyes?" he asked Morgan.

"Something that my father taught me a long time ago — but I'm no daddy's girl, so don't get it twisted," Morgan said before shifting back to him. "So Ramel I bet you were one of those mama's boys, weren't you? 'Yes mommy! No mommy!'"

"Honestly — yes. I honored my mother and her wishes," Ramel answered. "That's a good thing right? Don't women love a man who honors his mother?"

"Honor her? What does that mean? Because I'll have to say no if it means what I think it does," Morgan said in a serious tone.

"Honoring her means I treat you exactly like my mother taught me to treat a woman," he said satisfied with his own answer.

"So that means, you honor me, a high school dropout who left school for a nega who was beating my ass because I couldn't sell enough drugs for him at my high school! Really?" said a confused Morgan.

"Absolutely!! I see you as a woman worthy of my honor, Morgan. Can't believe you don't see that," he said with a curious frown.

"Anyway, give me ten minutes to jump in the shower, so I can buy you some breakfast before you head back home," he teased her with a smile and a kiss to her forehead.

While her "frequent sponsor" of all things pleasurable jumped in the shower, Morgan realized that she'd broken a cardinal rule: Never, ever let the sun catch you at a man's place.

She rushed out of bed, hopped in her little sundress, slid on her wedges, grabbed her cell phone, snatched her keys, and darted for his door.

"Front door is ajar!!!!!!!!" Ramel's alarm sounded off through his place. By then, Morgan was in a full sprint, popping her curvy, little hips down his driveway to her car as fast as her feet could take her.

Up until that moment, Ramel was basking in the glory of finally getting a hold of Morgan's lil' tight body, the right way. Indeed, he had been plotting and planning on that petite-ness for months.

But now, he's looking out of the second-floor window of his shower, watching Morgan scamper away quickly thinking, "What in the...what just happened? Morgan...Morgan...Baby, wait!" he sounded out. "Morgan, where are you going so fast, baby?"

Without a flinch of remorse, Morgan turned around and threw up her middle finger in his direction and never spoke to him again.

The silence spoke for a moment.

"What — in THE hell — just happened?" Ramel screamed out loudly looking at himself in the mirror. Crazily, Morgan was asking herself the same damn question, blazing 60 mph down a quiet neighborhood street at 6 a.m.

Ramel knew he hadn't done anything wrong. In fact, he probably had done everything right and exact. All their dealings were exciting: the wining and dining, the dancing, and outings, more importantly, the shopping sprees and mind-blowing sex!?! But what he wasn't aware of is that his biggest strengths were also his greatest downfalls with Morgan. Pardon all the good he'd done for her; Ramel was still a man. And, a man, her father David taught her years ago, is like a snake, never trust one.

CHAPTER 14

"... Ultimately, she'd turn her life into a movie ..."

Chase turned 19 shortly after graduation and chose to live the high life, a social media vixen for hire. She'd gained some power and made some money off the thirstiest negas on the internet. She controlled her destiny now, no longer under her mama's thumb or waiting on some random negas to supply her happiness. She'd found a few love affairs that kept pace with the rest of her fabulous life. Ultimately, she'd turn her life into a movie, now watch her shine.

—

On a beautiful 85-degree day in August, she watched one of her elaborate plans manifest. At 6pm sharp, a shining black chopper landed on a helipad on the rooftop of the Monuments' most exclusive hotel, The Maya. The door of the chopper swung open and all you could see was the legs of a former Black Beauty turned Black Goddess.

Had it not been for her mother constantly talking down on her, Chase could've very easily been a high-end model. Most ladies would kill for a set of legs like hers. She was rather tall for a girl, 5'7 nearly 5'11 in heels. Her legs are long and shapely, courtesy of long hours in the gym and extraordinarily little to no fried foods.

The pilot couldn't wait to hop and assist Chase down the short steps of the chopper. His eyes and mind fought a conflicting battle between quick glances and/or outright staring at her thighs, which seemed to be peaking at him every time she lifted a thigh to make another step down.

"Thank you kindly, sir!" she appreciated him, "oh, next time, you can stare — it's alright." Stunted, the chopper pilot couldn't say a word, just flashed a goofy smile.

Chase gracefully strolled across the rooftop, holding her wide-brim styled cream–colored hat close to her head, so it wouldn't blow away in the choppers breeze. The stylish hat matched a multicolored scarf perfectly, which blended very well with the brownish MK bag, her accessories, and the ankle strap heels.

John, her suitor, greeted her at the door with a hug and a soft kiss on her left hand. He swiped his card to enter the elevator which is hidden to 90% of The Maya's guests. The door opened and the doorman pushed the button one floor down. John was looking straight ahead seemingly, yet under his $1,500 shades, he was staring Chase up and down. She barely acknowledged him, ready to get to her honeycomb hideout for the weekend.

(The dong of an elevator bell sounds. "Penthouse floors," it says)

The doors opened to an upscale palatial palace for Chase to play in until Sunday night when she would fly back across town. Oh, you didn't know...yes, she has lived in Monument since birth, but so what? According to Chase, this was how power and love walk and talk. Please believe, she was not the least bit overwhelmed by the accommodations or shocked by the hospitality. She had come to expect it, especially dealing with John. Why? Because she perpetually owned him. Never mind that, we'll get to that later...

Back to the penthouse suite: Chase walked in, dropped her bag, and pointed the doorman where to place her Louis Vuitton luggage. Next, she sat on the side of the bed, and sighed comfortably. Still, she hadn't uttered a word to John yet. Her music playlist was already playing softly throughout the room, and you could smell the bubbles and hear the running waters of the jacuzzi.

Emotionlessly, she looked at John while she popped off her heels and threw her hat across the room. He completely recognized his role in all of this. Confidently, he walked over to Chase. She stood up seductively and turned her back away from him, pulled her braids aside, so he could unzip her dress. Slowly, he scrolled her zipper down her back to right above her ample apple bottom, then he gasped as he ran his hand across the design of her "tramp stamp". While he touched her, Chase backhanded his left cheek so hard her handprint was left on his face for a moment. Without missing a beat, she removed the dress from around her shoulders and allowed it to scantily hit the plush carpet exposing all her goodies.

There she was "bucket-naked" right in front of him as he stood there stuck not knowing whether to reach out and caress something or just stare at her awesomeness.

(His cell phones rings)

It was John's wife. Chase knew this because Chase knows his wife's ringtone. As he moved the phone to his ear to answer it, she walked slowly across the floor tantalizing him making it exceedingly difficult for him to speak. Chase purposely dropped her cell phone and bent over provocatively, providing him the perfect view of all her glory.

"Uh! Hey! Hey! What's open on ... I mean, I mean...What's going on?" John asked his wife.

His wife asked, "What's that music playing? Where are you, John? It's Friday evening, and I haven't heard from you since this morning?"

"I'm with a client trying to close on a deal," he responded.

"Oh, deal huh?" his wife scoffed.

"Let me call you back okay?" he suggested gingerly.

"Sure, but make sure you do that asap because lil' Cora has lost her damn mind," his wife added. "Lost her mind? How so?" John asked.

"She claimed her friend saw you at the airport in the helicopter hangar where her dad works earlier," his wife explained.

"Ah baby! That's crazy," John suggested, "why would I be there? Ha!"

"Oh really? That's the same thing I said until Cora's lil' friend took a pic of you and sent it to her phone," his wife added.

(Phone disconnected)

"Hello! Hello! I know she ain't just hanging up on me," John said.

John called back, but it went right to voicemail. He called several more times 'till he thought out loud, "She's probably calling the damn airport and getting all the information on the rental, the cost, who the riders were, and the destination of the chopper. I'm f*****!"

Meanwhile, Chase was carefree, just like she should be. Why is that? Because this was how the true divas, the she-bosses did it in the movies. Plus, she knew she owned Johnny-boy. How did she own him? Because she had the power to sink his business, his marriage, his heart, and his future happiness. At least, she convinced herself that she could if she wanted to.

John knew The Game, still he was a bit disturbed at this point. He knew how calculating his wife could be for one; for two, he knew she had the visual evidence to corroborate her story. On top of all that, their children were involved this time. She might have overlooked some private indiscretions, but she certainly won't tolerate this kind of disrespect in the eyes of her children without striking back in some form. Right then, John remembered what his Pops useta tell him: "You can sacrifice your whole kingdom with the wrong move, with the wrong person, at the wrong time."

"Oh John! Bring your simple ass in here," Chase shouted.

John sat down at the end of the bed for a moment. His heart started pounding, harder by the minute. Now, he realized this situation could go kaboom if the Mrs. showed up to see how he had Chase living, or to confront whichever bird he was caking because part of her money was financing Chase's fabulous weekend getaway. Perhaps, worse than that, Chase would leave him and cancel their future hot, steamy romantic episodes completely. Just then...

" John!" Chase shouted again.

"John! I know you hear me, cheap bastard?" Chase baited.

He walked in and found her sitting atop the rim of the jacuzzi, rubbing bubbles over her face, her neck, her stomach, and her legs, but leaving her most tempting private parts exposed to him in plain sight.

(His phone dropped and cracked on the floor.)

She rubbed more bubbles on her tummy and looked up at him like she was totally unaware of what she was doing and said, "Awe, Johnny–boy upset because wifey is hot on his trail?"

"Don't be like that, Chase," John remarked, "and please, don't scrap our weekend together with some of your selfishness."

Chase responded, still massaging her body a few feet from him, "Three things, Johnny boy. One, I don't give a frog's fat ass about your wife's feelings, BUT," she shouted, "you need to go home and fix that immediately. Why? Because you chose to play this game with me, and you will protect me from all drama if you want to have access to all of this."

She continued, "Two, have my room service sent up to me immediately because I'm getting hungry, and I want snacks to enjoy with my shows."

"And three, pass me the remote and my massager, so I'll have something to play with until you get your simple ass back here.

Mwah!"

She blew a kiss in his direction and slyly said, "See ya later …
Toodles!"

John gave Chase a small kiss on her cheek and avidly made his
move to deal with the fastly-approaching dramatic situation.

"... the ultimate gift and a curse ..."

"Thompson!!! Is that you?" Morgan said, pulling up on her old fling and the man you broke her best friend's heart.

"Mane — I see you've taken real good care of yourself since high school while many of our classmates are spreading out like a can of biscuits. You - you still got that basketball-star glow though," she continued, smiling from ear to ear.

"Morgan! I have been doing my thing in the gym, yaknow? My whole life changed after you. Everything I did, everything I was, and everything I've become since then has been your influence."

"Boy, you need to quit," Morgan deflected.

"No seriously! The Shebas I dealt with after you were like catching small three-pound catfish after bagging a 20-pound Red Snapper; there's just no comparison, is it? And you still acknowledged me and showed me love after all these years. Wow!" Thompson finished.

"Bahahahahahahaha...the big red snapper!!! Boy Stop!" Morgan joked.

"See...see how you do? See, how you get a man going, Morgan?" Thompson joked.

"Boy please, we're both grown now, so I know you ain't

falling for my lines, so stop it. Plus, you know I'm just joking with you," Morgan slickly replied.

"Nah, babygirl, guys aren't supposed to admit this EVER but — but you turned me out," Thompson said.

"Hell, I'm probably still turned out, but for some reason, you never see the effects you have on others, do you Morgan?"

"Man, get on gone with that talk," Morgan giggled, "I'm just me."

"Yep, you are," Thompson retorted, "the ultimate gift and a curse."

"En-tee-ways!" Morgan replied.

"What can I do for you, babygirl?" asked Thompson.

"Lunch? Dinner? Either one," she said. "We need to talk business?"

"Business and/or pleasure, or just business because I'm taking off on Friday for the holiday. What's best for you?" he asked.

"Well hell you know me, ain't no real business unless I'm getting some pleasure out of it. How about lunch at hmm, Brother El's spot on Broad? Let's say like 11:30am?" she suggested.

Thompson replied, "Perfec. Good talking to you, Morg. I'll hit you up."

"Same here, mane. I'll see you on Friday," she continued.

As Morgan slithered back down the block, she hit up Dani

immediately.

"Hey Girl! Let's hit the hair store, so I can get you right, it's going down with you and Thompson on Friday, Boo-Boo," Morgan said with a chuckle.

"Oh Gawd, Morg! What did you do, Biscuit?" Dani inquired.

"We'll talk when I get there, mane." Morgan laughed and swiped left on the cell.

"We bout to get this nega, mane!" Morgan laughed herself.

—

"Okay, now! So, I saw that nega Thompson at the mall earlier today, right?" Morgan shared with her bestie.

"Oh Gawd," Dani frowned, "why did you have to bring him up? You know I always overthink everything. Now, I must go through all the why's and how's and what's, ifs, and if nots with you again. Ugh!"

"Hoe-sit-down!" Morgan always said when anyone was cutting up.

"Listen lil' girl, you could've just listened to me, but nooooooo! Thompson was — so — so tall — so fine — so popular. You were so surprised he liked you. A whole lot of this and that, we're not going through that again. This is the big payback!" Morgan chided.

"I know, Morg," Dani said, "he was so dreamy back then, but I wish he'd get torn to pieces by four rabid pit bulls and not die either, so his ass can suffer."

"Mane never mind all that there, you do know I still got 'em eating out of my hands. He was standing there looking all thirsty ... hanging on my every word ... begging me for another shot, even after he did you like that!" Morgan paused a second.

"And?" Dani asked. "Did you cuss his knock-kneed ass out?"

"Nope! I got his number, Danielle!" Morgan responded with an evil grin.

"What for? Oh, my Gawd," Dani responded sounding like an innocent, but curious schoolgirl. "Where are you going with all of this?"

CHAPTER 16

"Keep the cash. Keep the rose. "

Coming out of the hair store, Morgan collided with a well-known hustler named Stone, aka Well-known Stone. Stone was an ex-street pharmacist, who served a dime and came home with a legitimate hustle that put him right back on top. He connected with the right negas on the inside and had better merchandise on the street than some department stores. He was dropping by Mae Lings Hair spot in the hood to drop off Moorish oils and designer wardrobe for the back of her store, when he ran into the green-eyed man-killer.

It was fashionable that Morgan didn't bat an eye at Stone, at least not an eye he'd notice this time. As she swam through the premium bundles to hook Dani's head up, Morgan bargained with Mae Ling. The two of them go way back because Mae Ling owned the nail shop next door, and Morgan hits that spot faithfully every two weeks.

"Mama Sue, is this young lady bothering you?" Stone asked, speaking about Morgan.

In classic Asian form, Mae Ling smiled and smirked but never said a mumbling word to Stone or Morgan. Plus, she was getting money with the two of them, so she wasn't creeping into their conversation.

"Listen, young gal, you must be one of those little thotties from Monument, huh?" he asked her in a condescending tone.

Morgan never acknowledged a word he said. So, cleverly, Stone pulls out a stack rolled up in a rubber band and lays it on the top of her huge Gucci Bag. He stepped back to measure her reaction. Always a gangsta, Morgan slid the money down in her purse grabbed the most expensive bundle and headed to the counter.

"Wait a minute ...," Stone said, walking up behind her.

Morgan quickly turned towards Stone and pulled out the Glock 9 and screamed, "Mane, don't run up on me! If you're sharing bread then share it. Be about that life or be out of my face!"

Stone grabbed his money bags, merchandise, and told Mama Sue, "I'll see ya next time, ya dig?" He glanced back at Morgan, shook his head, and walked out the door. Now, of course, he waited for Morgan to come outside. When she did, he snatched a single rose from the flower shop next door and presented to her. "Please forgive me Shawty. Keep the cash. Keep your rose. Keep your name even. Let me get your number, and we'll call it even."

Morgan reached in his pocket and pulled out his phone, told him to unlock it, punched in her numbers, handed him the phone back, popped her gum and sashayed so seductively down the block.

Mae Ling's son and Stone's business partner Jet asked Stone, "Mane, I've been crushing on her for years. Are you on that now?"

"I don't know J, but we're about to be on it hard!" Stone said biting his lip and watching her walk her sexy self-down the block.

" ... random jobs, random hoes, random problems ..."

All the romantic comedies and urban thrillers with love interest coupled with real life, game-time experiences have given Chase a certain amount of knowledge to draw from for the future. Indeed, her awesome episodes of love, adventure, and danger had fed her wanting spirit a lot more than the insecure, self-esteem destroying nonsense her mother fed her as a youth. But her attraction powers and unique beauty brought her another type of livelihood dealing with the guys.

Rashid's life is a question mark. He had random jobs, random hoes, random problems, but never found any real solutions. Jobs do not hire big black negas. Period. Big black negas don't have money for therapists to even talk about their problems, let alone solutions. Then, there's the hoes. He thinks he's on top of his pimp game, but after five children and two baby mothers, it's obvious he's deluded as hell. But then, he met Chase.

Chase was rapid-fire lust, a lunar scorpion. She had styles upon styles upon styles to how she dressed. Her words were as colorful as her speech. Rashid liked those big booty Shebas, and though Chase had a nice cinnamon colored apple, it wasn't a stupid booty. But hell, there's no way you could tell because her hips sang melodies as she walked, and Rashid got caught up "checking out her melody."

She froze him. Literally; he stood frozen in his tracks. So much so, he dared not have a conversation with her unless he was crushed out heavenly.

"I thought we were going to brunch at the Marriot today, Rashid?" she asked.

Rashid responded, "Hold up, I told you that was on if my baby-moms came to pick up my kids! Her trifling ass probably sensed I was trying to get out because..."

"Wait nega?" Chase quickly cut him off. "That's because she knew your simple ass got paid yesterday. Right? Right?"

"Look Chase, I ain't hearing it today. I ain't in the mood. Plus, she just got me for $400 for the damn power bill," a vexed Rashid answered.

"So, I ain't in the mood to hear about no $55 a plate brunch that you're upset that we didn't go too. I got real problems, girl!" Rashid added.

"Nega, I know you ain't spent my money on your kids," Chase retorted shockingly. "Oh wait, not your kids, but you spent my brunch money on your fat-ass baby moms power bill?"

"Wait! Hold up? What's more important?" he asked her.

Quickly, Chase shot back another clever question, "What's more important or what's more important to me, nega?"

Rashid responded, "Yo, you know what? If we gotta take it

there, let's take it all the way there. What is more important to you, Chase?"

"Wait, you're going to twist your lips to ask me that, Rashid? Really? You really have to ask me that?" Chase asked in disbelief.

"Of course, not" Rashid said, "I already know the answer. In your mind, only one thing in the world is important... "

"Me!" Chase yelled.

"You are!" Rashid shouted.

"Damn right I am, since you wanna take it there Rashid!" she further explained.

"Huh? Really?" he asked. "What'd you say? You're more important than my kids having lights and hot water in the house? You are a super disrespectful man."

Chase shook a head slightly like she had a dizzy spell then smiled at Rashid. She walked up to him and stood on her tippy toes as if to whisper in his ear. "As long as daddy keeps serving this up to lil' mama every time she needs it, you'll have no problems out of me," all the while grabbing his formidable package.

As he stood there dazed and gazing into her eyes, he didn't realize he had just been had. When placed in a tight situation, The Game had taught Chase to retreat to safer ground immediately.

Rashid's antics brought "ole Johnny-Boy" to mind.

Remember, John was put on the shelf after the near run-in with his wife about the helicopter, the penthouse, and the photos of him taken by his daughter's friend. Cleverly, Chase thought it would be the perfect time to bring John off the shelf for some shopping exploits. Plus, he had texted her earlier that day, like he did every day since the breakup, to assure her that he was available for her needs. Now, back to Rashid...

"Baby, Rashid, you know I'm not that shallow. It's all about your kids. Don't ever doubt that!" Chase intimated, quickly switching up her position.

"Damn baby! I knew that you'd think about this good wood, and it'll remind you do not go off the deep end. You know how I get down, when I do what I do ya' know?" an arrogant Rashid stated.

"Mmmmhmmmm baby, you're all I'll ever need," Chase said emphatically. "Hey babe! I know I've made your day stressful, and I apologize for my selfishness. I should give you some time with your kids, but I need a favor first?"

A puffed-up Rashid hit his blunt again and asked, "Oh yeah! So, what can daddy do for lil' mama?"

"First, bless me with the El-D! Second, I want you to drop me off at the Metro, so I can let you smoke, choke, and relax after this stress reliever." Chase asked slyly.

CHAPTER 18

"I took full advantage of the situation ..."

Here's my current situation: career-wise, my babies are still the most precious things in my life. However, it seemed assisting them with love and relationships only opened a trick bag of more problems. Still, I serve as their coolest mentor and their Auntie Bey forever.

What else? Well, the Most High took my mama and daddy from me at the same damn time. How cruel was that? Hell, I am Esther Bey. It was not fair! I started to consider whether I was cursed to live out my remaining days as a Random. I thought so, then Thomas showed up. That man of God genuinely cared for me. Plus, it had been a long time since any man had made me feel that way.

Did I ever mention I'm a Solar Libra with a Venus in Cancer? That might not mean a lot to you but to those in the know, know! It simply means that my intuition is keen and allows me to see what kind of whirlwind I had caused in the Pastor Thomas' home. The fact that he sparsely returned texts and never returned my calls unless he was on church grounds let me know the proverbial poo-poo had hit the fan. And so what? What else am I supposed to hold on to?

The past 48 hours for the Good Reverend Doctor have been crappy at best. His wife Joy has been deeply hurt by his recent actions and is starting to question whether she can ever trust him again. Finally, the time has come for both to make some tough decisions. The pastor must decide on being faithful to his flock—mainly me—or allow peace to reign in his home.

—

It was 4:30 pm, one half hour away from his next counseling session with Esther Bey. As always, he eased out of the lazy boy chair, laid out his clothes on the bed, and headed for the shower. Immediately, Joy jumped up too, laid out her clothes too, and hopped in the shower right after he finished up. As he dressed, she dressed too. When he left heading towards the church, she followed behind him in her luxury vehicle. Still, they hadn't said one word to one another. He pulled into the pastor's parking space, she pulled into the spot for the first lady right next to his. He entered the sanctuary, strolled into his office, shut the door behind him. The First Lady walked in right behind him yet chose to sit in the waiting area of the office to chat with the secretary. Joy craftily acted as if nothing at all was going on between her and the pastor.

—

After about fifteen minutes or so before our session, I sounded the bell from the outside door. The secretary checked the monitor and buzzed me in. Knowing what I was facing, I took full advantage of the situation and wore a skintight blue denim catsuit with brown pumps and a brown Louis Vuitton bag. I had a long ponytail that set atop my perfectly round donk.

Indeed, I strolled into the church's office with the confidence of a runway model at a high-class fashion show. My hips swayed back and forth as if they were in perfect accord with my flat waistline making a circular motion with every step I took.

"Hey Miss Pearl! I'm here for my weekly appointment," I said fervently, staring into the glaring eyes of the First Lady. Just then, Joy leaned back in her seat and crossed her legs, I guess to let me know my antics weren't moving her at all.

Silently yet taking in every word, Ms. Pearl kept her secretary duties going while watching this charade take place.

"Pastor!" she said, "Miss Bey is here."

"Very good, very good. I'll be right there," he replied.

He quickly opened his door and attempted to greet me in a respectable fashion, but he couldn't get out a word.

"Ah- ah-ah-hello, Ms. Bey," he said, stuttering.

I replied, "Hello Thomas!

"Excuse me, Madame First Lady," I nodded, waltzing right by her and right into her husband's office.

Though he tried to remain tactful, he couldn't help but stare at my ample rear as I moved slowly toward the visitor's chairs in his office. Once he realized he was totally mesmerized and in a deep, deep stare he stupidly gathered himself, smiled, then turned toward his wife and promptly slammed his door shut.

((((((Wham))))))

After 45 minutes or so, Thomas was trying his best to listen to my concerns, but I made sure bubbling boobs were staring back at him.

"Pastor, I'm starting to feel really vulnerable. I need someone or something to hold, touch, and comfort me during this time," I revealed. "I lie in bed at night yearning for...for...for something that...that...that ..."

"Yes! Okay. Can you explain the—'that'?" he said sliding up in his seat.

"I don't know exactly what that is, Pastor. I figured you could offer some suggestions as to whom or what I need in my life because I think we know the why. And then how to make this deep emptiness go away?" I begged, tears welling up in my eyes.

"Sister Esther," he said, looking exasperated from dealing with his divine duty and his lust. "We will find a solution soon enough. I think? The point is to keep seeking that divine way that will bring healing and wholeness."

At that moment, I stood to my feet and started to parade through the office trying to further flaunt, I mean, explain my emptiness. While I walked, I slapped my thighs and butt at times to emphasize my point. I posted my hand on my hips sashaying from side to side. Then, I finally walked over to him and sat on the desk while rubbing my feet against his leg.

"Sister Bey," Pastor said, "I think it would be wise if you would move back to the other side of the desk.

((((((Knock! Knock! Knock!))))))

The First Lady Joy had had enough. She'd been as patient as she possible could, and now it was time get to him and her straight.

The pastor opened the door.

"How long is this session anyway?" the First Lady said selfishly.

Pastor Thomas slammed the door in her face again without saying a word.

"Thomas! Thomas! Open this door," she screamed, before realizing how embarrassing her actions had become. She summoned her dignity and walked away.

—

Miss Pearl, the faithful secretary, was steadily taking notes and texting the word out as it was happening. After Pastor and I parted ways, he stayed in the office for hours. I left unfulfilled, yet happy that I exploited the First Lady with my petty antics.

Little did we know that the past hour would shape the four of our lives drastically in the coming months.

For one, Pastor Thomas was heralded as a weak unfaithful man, yet a great and faithful servant of the white Jesus that hung above his office desk.

Two, his wife became known as a bonafide ride-or-die wife who was ready to scrap for her husband because he wouldn't put his hoe in check.

Three, Miss Pearl became Monument City's new Wendy Williams, commanding all the latest, hot, juicy topics from the fornicating, drunken, LGBT-community supported activities going on in the sanctuary.

And bringing up the rear, me—you know, the woman who just buried her mother and father by herself without the emotional support of any living relatives. I became the pastor's prostitute and the so-called whore of the Zion Methodist Church. All because my actions in the office that day were not only heard, but viewed on the camera that sits under Miss Pearl's desk. So, she and the first lady saw and heard every word that was going on.

Consequently, I left the church shortly afterwards without resolving any of her issues.

CHAPTER 19

"Good-bye!"

It was Morgan's 18th birthday weekend. Dani and the rest of her girlfriends had the party of all parties planned. It was a who's-who guest list including Morgan's king for the evening, Stone, and his ruff-neck crew. In the words of the unstoppable Puff Daddy, "Why don't my friends, link with your friends, and yeah we could do this every night!" Sounds like makings of an epic night, but little did Morgan know she'd be the "odd-one out" on her 18th G-Day.

Although Stone tried his damnest to renegotiate some out of state business with Asian J, it was a no-go: too much product and too much money to be made. Stupidly, Stone waited until the night before Morgan's party to Facetime her the untimely news.

"Stone, what's up, mane? I mean what the hell! Where you been at, babe?" Morgan asked.

"I've been building a new bridge for the one I'm about to burn down right now," Stone responded.

"Huh? What does that mean?" asked Morgan. "Mane, I could give a damn about some other gal mane...SO.... what are you talking about? Somebody pregnant? Somebody seriously ill?"

Awnah, baby! All I wanted to say is we are heading to Jamaica first thing Monday morning!" Stone said stammering.

"Stone, stop friggin playing with me, mane? What that got to do with burning some damn bridge or something?" Morgan asked in nasty tone.

"I need you to start packing and pick me up from the Northside Airport on Sunday afternoon, okay baby?" Stone asked nervously.

"Oh ok, so we're leaving next Monday, not Monday coming up...because ummm...my damn 18th birthday party is that deal tomorrow night," said an excited Morgan.

Their silence spoke for a moment.

An obviously aggravated Morgan questioned him, "Stone, why ain't you looking at me when you're talking? Da'hell is up mane. Ohhhh!!! You slick like telling me you ain't going to be here for the biggest party of my life!!!?"

Knock! Knock! Knock! (Someone is at her hotel door)

"Hold on mane! Somebody is at my door. You better get yourself together quick before I get back," Morgan said leaving her phone to answer the door. She opened the door and found Darren, Stone's brother, smiling back at her.

"What up sis? Big bro told me to drop these off to you," he said, passing her the package.

"Hey! Hey! Hold that elevator please. Aight Morg!," he said trotting back down the hotel's long hallway.

Morgan returned to her iPhone with a manila envelope in hand. "Mane, what da'hell you told Darren to bring over here at this time of the night?" her face drooping as she inquired.

"Why didn't you just bring this here? Where are you at right now, Stone?" she asked.

Stone said, "I'm at a hotel, of course. Can't you see the background? Oh yeah, Asian J says wassup?"

"Asian J! He's in there with you? Wait! What?! You're in a hotel...where nega? Here, in town, right?" she asked again.

Stone dropped his head and mumbled, "Nah babe! I'm not there, Suga Plum."

"So where are you at?" Morgan asked again. "In a hotel room, where?"

Stone kept his head down and remained quiet for the moment.

"I mean if it's with another chick, that's you and Li's business, but what's good with your location?" Morgan asked again.

"I'm in a hotel in Philly, Morgan baby," breaking his silence, "and I won't be back until..."

(Morgan picked up her lighter)

"Until...Wait! What are you doing with that lighter, babe?" he pleaded.

"Wait...Really mane!" she said calmly, yet deadly serious.

Morgan politely walked into the bathroom, set her phone down on the sink, placed the manila envelope inside of the huge sink, rear-faced her camera so he could see exactly what was going on, and set it on fire. As soon as the last piece of the envelope turned to ashes, she front-faced the camera, whipped her falling tears and said, "Goodbye!"

CHAPTER 20

"You portrayed yourself as trophy and I played you like one."

It was time to put Dani's plans in motion. Gone were the days of being the Trophy Girlfriend. Gone were the days of expecting to find Prince Charming. Gone were the days of giving her heart to every cute, yet weak-minded mind man that she eventually desired to control and manipulate. Hello to the days when bitterness, hatred, and vengeance ruled Dani's every thought.

She'd studied the texts and interactions of how every relationship started, reached it apex, and then failed miserably. She could literally pass a test on the who's, when's, what's, and the where's of how each guy took unfair advantage of her. Now, she's tired of complaining to this person or that person about her troubled past and, more than ever, she's tired of Morgan coaching her on how scary and dull she was to have never voiced her opinion to these negas who did her wrong in the first place. In between failed relationships, she met yet another unsuspecting, guy got pregnant, and forced him to marry her immediately.

So, Dani finally had a little footing—or so she thought. She forced a pregnancy, pushed a marriage, then tried to guilt the man into loving her or at least, doing what she told him to do.

Well, karma's a bitch, and it was time for this bitch to bite.

Morgan happily sacrificed herself so her A-1 from Day-1 could exorcise vengeance on one of the males who broke her heart. Never mind the fact that Dani had a whole husband at home and a youngen to raise, Thompson still owned a huge piece of her heart's real estate. And this was the perfect situation for Morgan's Gemini soul to cleanse itself after her 18th birthday fiasco without Stone.

Taking a slick tip from the movie, *You've Got Mail*, Morgan told Thompson to meet her at a restaurant. She said there will be a reserved table that had roses and a copy of *The Coldest Winter Ever* sitting on it. She also instructed him to buy a bottle of Chardonnay and have a glass poured for her when she arrived.

Thompson couldn't refuse Morgan. Why? Because Morgan had that kind of sexual Mojo that made her suns do exactly what she requested of them. No one knows whether it was her beauty that commanded that type of respect, or the way she asked. Besides all that, it worked.

"There he is, Dani," Morgan said, sitting behind dark tints in a SUV outside of the restaurant.

"Oh My God, I am so torn right now," Dani said.

"Bird, why?" Morgan asked. "This is your chance."

"Chance to what?" Dani inquired.

"The chance to confront one of these clowns who broke your heart into a thousand pieces," Morgan challenged.

"Yeah, I guess it is," Dani replied.

"Nah, Dani!" Morgan retorted. "We know it is. Let's get it. You remember what we talked about now?"

"Yes! No fears and most definitely no tears," Dani said.

"You better not, ya big cry baby," Morgan joked, making her burst out in laughter.

"Thank you! I needed that chuckle," Dani said, closing the door shut.

Dani's style was ethnic for the showdown: earth tones and Senegalese braids. Her wrap dress fit her snugly, exposing the extra thick curves that had tightened and toned from high school. She saw her reflection as she approached the door, deciding to fix her hair one last time, check her makeup, and pull down the snug dress closer to her knees.

His back was to her, so he didn't notice her approaching, but as she reached the table, he said, "Wait...umm...What are you doing here, Danielle? Right here? Right now? On the same exact day and time, I'm supposed to be meeting your bestie..."

"Bastard please, will you sit down first?" Dani shot back. If she was nervous and fighting back tears and anxiety, then those feelings went south as soon as he came out of his mouth wrong.

"I think you know exactly what it is...now," Dani said with much attitude. "You're a smart guy."

"Smart enough that you couldn't plan this interaction

alone, Miss Choir girl," Thompson retorted. "Nah, this has Morgan written all over it."

"Are you kidding me?" Dani shot back quickly, "not only am I a lame choir girl, I guess I'm slow too, huh?"

"Where is Morgan? And why are you here? Period. Point blank." Thompson said. "I was looking forward to seeing one of the loves of my life and ended up seeing one of the duds from my life."

"Oh, you went all the way there huh? You black, long lipped bastard?" Dani said.

"Ha!" Thompson chuckled, "you remember you called my cell and sung 'That's What Friends Are For' on my answering machine? I shared every voice message you left me with the whole basketball team on the way to our games. We useta laugh hysterically at how pathetic you were. Begging, begging, and begging and at the same time thinking you were better than every other bird I chirped with because you were a church girl."

"So, what I always thought was the problem was actually it, huh?" Dani asked. "You just wanted to crack open the sacred legs of the good church girl. I was a virgin when you started telling me your lies. I gave you my everything, ya black bastard..."

"Wait! It wasn't much..." Thompson interrupted her.

"...Well whatever..." Dani responded, "why didn't you just tell me the truth? Why would you play me like that? Why would you use me for my time and love just to use and exploit me to all your friends and the basketball team and coaches—oh my god ....why?"

"Because that's what negas do to Trophies!" Thompson said emphatically. "You portrayed yourself as Trophy and I played you like one. End of story...anything else?"

"You friggin' bastard," Dani answered, "I had my reasons why you did what you did, but I also got reasons for..."

Right then, Dani pulled a survivor's knife out of her Coach bag and quickly put it to his eye, leaned in closer and said, "Muthafuggah if I ever see you again, this right eye is mine."

"Bird, you're coo-coo crazy," Thompson yelled through the restaurant.

"Yeah, I might be, but come outta hiding again, and that eye will be a trophy in a jar," she said as she dashed out the place, heels in hand, and headed for Morgan's ride. Morgan peeped her coming with a much speed and cranked up the engine, pushed open the passenger door and away they went down Dauphin Street.

"... we don't have anything, but tomato soup and grilled cheese sandwiches."

Thirty minutes later, Chase was riding shotgun heading to the Metro laying out her next movement smoothly.

Snapchat + Twitter + Instagram =

#onthemove #notime4fake1s #boybegone #on2danext #wheredareal1s@

(Text from John comes in immediately)

Chase: Hey

John: What's up?

Chase: Meet me at the Hillsdale Metro in thirty minutes! And bring a six pack please?"

John: ... a six pack of? Brews?

Chase: Nah boyee, Magnums!!!!

John: Say no more.

Chase: Cool.

Just then, Rashid asked, "Babe, who's scooping you up from the Metro? You know I can take you home if you want?"

"Oh, uh, nah! I'm good, baby, you go and get your rest. My cousin Jonathan is in town this weekend, and we were supposed to do something after our brunch, but we can just do it now," Chase answered.

"Aight! Here we are," said Rashid.

"Yes, we are. Gimme a kiss! Thanks baby," Chase answered. "Call me when you wake up, lovey!"

"Alright! I will," said an eager Rashid speeding off the Metro lot.

Chase's phone vibrates again as soon as she closes the car door.

(Chase receives another text from John)

John: I'm on my way now...

Chase: Just lovely...

———

Twenty minutes later, Rashid arrived at Dina's crib with $60 worth of groceries. He was swamped at the door by Dina's four boys, none of which were his, yet and still he was treated like the king of their castle.

Dina came out wearing Rashid's University of Alabama football jersey, draped over her like a dress. She fixed his plate while he played PS4 with the young cubs.

"They were so happy to hear that you were coming over, " Dina said excitedly.

"Ain't nothing or no one going to keep me away from y'all

Baby-Dee," Rashid stated. "Besides how can I stay away when all you do is love on me?!"

"Rashid, don't do that? I don't really have anything else to offer you, but my love...my heart...and these crazy boys of mine," she said bashfully.

She continued, "By the way, we don't have anything, but tomato soup and grilled cheese sandwiches."

"And!!!" Rashid snapped back at her. "Please don't make me feel that way Dina—that sounds delicious. Besides, as you see we got a few groceries now. Plus, I will bring more tomorrow."

A single tear fell from her eye as she quickly turned and walked back to put the food away.

"Nah, Nah, Nah, wait! What's this I'm seeing right now?" Rashid asked, putting down his bowl and half a sandwich.

"I ain't trying to let you see me like this. I don't have anything to offer you, Rashid? Not nothing real," she suggested again.

"Oh, you don't? Come here for a minute," he said, as he grabbed her hand and headed towards her bedroom.

"Hey man!" Rashid yelled, but wearing a smile, "I know y'all ain't eat my whole sandwich that fast. And I see who sucked down my soup."

The boys laugh at their brother who now has hot tomato soup splattered all over his fresh white tee.

"Never mind them," Dina said.

Rashid opened Dina's bedroom door and commenced to pull her in the room by the bottom of his Alabama jersey. He sang softly, "Sweet home Alabama!"

"Wait, wait, what are you doing to me, boyee?" Dina giggled.

"Loving you!" he said, with a corny smirk, "now love me back!"

CHAPTER 22

Dani sat reminiscing about the hard times she had with her grandmother and how her Granny always made it better. Her husband walked in from a flag football league and caught the satisfied smirk on her face.

"So—what's on your little mind, Danielle? Money or money?" he said laughing slyly.

"Thinking back over my life, and all I've done since Granny passed. I wish she could see me now!" Dani told her husband.

"Why is that?" he asked suspiciously. "What did you do but drop out of school to come home and raise babies!?"

"WOW! Are you kidding me? Is that all you think of me after giving you your first son?" she asked regretfully.

"Look—I love my boy. He is everything to me, but I can't stand the sight of you, Dani," he said angrily.

"Well, that's hurtful, you nothing-ass-bastard!!" she said that the top of her voice.

He shouted back, "I mean let's be real. You forced me to marry you because of him, not because we had done anything more than—"

"What? Say it you bastard! I'll make sure your son will hate you forever. Say it!" Dani said.

"All we've ever done is bone, Dani! And to be perfectly honest, it's just here and available—it ain't good by any stretch of the imagination."

"I guess that's why you're always on your phone with something better, huh?" she said, face contorting, holding back tears. Dani turned to walk out of the room.

"Mmmmh! Is that it? Did the big bad man hurt her feelings?" he taunted her.

She turned around slowly back in his direction. "Umm no! You ain't big bad nothing," she said, looking at his crotch. Let me tell you something. I watched how you grew up. How nasty your family treated you? You treated me like you had been taught. Funny thing is, it never really hurt because my daddy never cared for me at all."

———

Several months or so after her birthday fiasco, Morgan met a new guy named Daquan. Daquan was friends with her ghetto botanist aka her weed man, former abuser, and employer Quincy. Quincy, or Que for short, told Morgan to slide past his crib to cook some plants and speak on all things urban and political. As she sat with the two of them, the ever-nonchalant Morgan started to scout Daquan like a general manager overseeing some new talent, yet he never had a clue he was under her scope.

Now, Daquan was not as tall as she liked her boy-toys, not as cut-up either, but he caught her off guard with his "idgafabout-nothing-or-no-one" personality. Daquan was mega-sarcastic and rude, but a gentleman at the same time. Again, Morgan was a June baby, so she loved the spontaneity of his October conversation and thought he'd be a nice new project for her to play with for a while. Remember, in Morgan's mind, Randoms are like utilities: use them at one's discretion.

After the smoke from cooking plants had filled the air in Que's crib, the three of them decided to hit the corner store for the "proper smacked snacks." The plants had them extremely lazy but growing ferociously hungry, so the "lazy drivers committee" had an impromptu meeting over which car to take.

"Nega don't even ask me because I just got here," Morgan stated emphatically.

"So, what Shawty? That just means your whip is still warmed up," Daquan chimed in, shaking his head at Morgan.

Immediately, Que stopped the feud, "For real! I'll drive. Now, let's get to it, please. Y'all ackin' like kids for real."

So, Morgan hopped in the backseat. Daqaun rode shotgun. Que slid behind the wheel and as soon as he stuck his key in the ignition, a car bent the corner and headed full speed in their direction. The car darted in front of Que's and parked blocking them in.

"Uh-oh!" Que said softly as if he knew the drama was coming.

"Uh-oh, what, bwoy?" Daquan asked before looking up.

"Ah hawl, hell nawl. Tell me that ain't Keisha in the car?"

Daquan uttered under his breath.

"Man yes it is! Oh well, here we go?" Que said.

"Who in the hell is Keisha?" a playful yet clueless Morgan asked.

By the way, Morgan loved these types of situations. Whereas some females would be nervous riding with two guys when a car filled with angry females pulled up, Morgan sat up and flashed her "it's-about-to-go-down" smile.

(Brakes have screeched. Doors have slammed. Now, the sounds of heels click hard across the pavement.)

"Hey girl, don't come over starting chaos," Que yelled.

"Boy...hush!! Daquan's goofy ass left his keys at the house before he headed over here," Keisha claimed, rudely reaching over Que to pass Daquan his keys.

"Keisha Chaos, why didn't you just walk around to the other side of the car instead of reaching all past that man's face like that? Damn! You just super disrespectful at times," said a surly Daquan.

"Oh, nega please, I'm just trying to make sure you can get back into my apartment because I'll be helping out at the baby shower all day," Keisha responded.

"Thank you, but ummm...yeah bye Keisha!," Daquan yelled in a nasty tone.

Stooping down and peeking into the back seat now, the ever-suspicious Keisha is just staring into Morgan's face, while the carefree Morgan is staring back at her like "this-ain't-what-you-want".

"Oh, my bad," said Que, "Keisha, this is Morgan. Morgan, that's crazy Keisha, Daquan's burden, I mean his Queen Bee," as he smirked.

"Good to meet you, babygirl!" Morgan said with a huge Kool-aid, extra playful smile.

"Hmmm? Oh! I'm so sure, Miss thang," Keisha responded.

"Miss Thang?! Mane bye!" Morgan yelled back.

The two of them stopped for a minute, sizing each other up until one of Keisha's friends told her to get her "messy ass" back in the car.

"As soon as her door slammed and they peeled off, Keisha stuck her head out of the door and yelled, "Bye then, Punk Ass!!!"

Morgan, never missing an opportunity to be messy chimed right in, "Damn nega! You let ya' old lady carry you like that," before she burst out in laughter.

"Mind yours, Lil' Bit, would you? By the way, she was talking to you when she yelled out the car door," Daqaun shot back at her.

"...telling them not to fall in love, and the more I say it..."

Morgan was across town dodging all kinds of calls and texts from her other Randoms. Daquan had this spark about him, and she liked it...a lot. Too many guys threw themselves at her all the damn time, so the mere fact he didn't seem to care about her at all raised her curiosities. Plus, she didn't care for the way Daquan's old lady, Keisha, tried to handle her at their last meeting. To be honest, that's really what had her hooked. Keisha's attitude towards her gave her all the gas she needed to jump-start her interest.

As these thoughts swirled around her crafty, sinister mind, her Auntie Ivey perceived some devilishness building around her. Ivey, a cosmic reader, had been telling her that she'd seen something strange in her cards lately.

"OG Ivey!!! You keep sending me these random messages with the same tarot card, what does this card mean?" asked Morgan.

"Morgan, baby, I know you THINK you have thangs under control," Ivey said, "still, it's a big, wide, world out there, and everything we suffer through ain't always somebody else's fault. Yaundeestandmeh?"

"I mean, damn Auntie...I'm sayin' though, in terms of what?" Morgan's tone became more and more aggravated by the moment. "I mean what you are talkin' 'bout, for real for real?"

"I'm talking in terms of how you deal with these lil' boys and how y'all go-through, yall go-through," Ivey responded.

"Oh, you are talking about dudes. I apologize that a few of them done got stupid with you, but I cleaned that up. They won't be coming to your front door no mo' though," Morgan assured her.

"And, that ain't all. They don't call my house phone and that darn, darn...um, um, whatchamacallit .... lil' girl," said Ivey with a chuckle.

"Oh...you mean your cell phone," Morgan added, "Hehehehehehehehe!!!"

"I don't even know how to work like that and you trying to show me how to block calls and silence them. Child please, I'm too old for all that mess," Ivey responded in a jovial way.

"Yeah, Auntie, I am telling them not to fall in love, and the more I say it the more they fall for me!" Morgan responded.

"And see..there...right there!" Ivey cut her off.

"What?" Morgan asked.

"That's where your problem begins and ends," said Ivey.

"See, that's why ion' be...umm...wait...how in the world is that my fault when I tell them that I am not fully available for them from the jump?" asked an exasperated Morgan.

"It's all in your technique, which is why I keep drawing this card as it relates to you," Ivey claimed.

"Auntie, I just sit here outta respect. You know I don't believe in any of that mess. Wait! No. Not a mess. It's hard to believe how some card, or my sign or my birth order, or my number, is going to tell me how my life is going to be lived," answered a clueless looking Morgan.

"So, where do your answers come from then, babygirl?" Ivey asked.

"From me?" Morgan claimed.

"Foolish. And that's why all these damn boys arrive at my doorstep or blow up my phone cuz your...your...umm... what's that y'all say, oh cuz ya' game ain't tight, ha-ha," Ivey added in a real, but sarcastic way.

"But listen for a second, this lil' card is called The Hanged Man. It's placed in reverse, so as it relates to love it's telling me more than you ever would yourself," Ivey claimed.

"Hmm. How so?" Morgan asked just feeding into her mindset now.

"So," Ivey began to explain, "Here's the card, look at it. No chile, look at it good. Its theme is talking about 'letting go'."

Morgan stopped her, "Letting go...letting go of what? My negas. Really? All of them?"

"Well, you may need to 'let go' of a certain kind of relationship. You have to stop thinking the only way that you can be happy is getting these boys caught up in your net and pulling them out as you want to see them."

"See, I don't know about that Auntie," Morgan insisted, "because that's how you taught me to play the game."

"I get that baby, really I do. But who do you see 'round here with me now?" Ivey asked.

"Nobody really, especially since Senior got hitched," Morgan answered.

"Exactly! Someone told me once that 'the babies are the best part,' so I'm doing my best to steer you away from the mess I might have brought you into, Yaundeestandmeh?" Ivey added.

Morgan laughed, "Aight! Ha-ha! If we're clear, and you ain't being no hypocrite then we're good, Ivey, please proceed."

They both burst out in laughter for a few minutes and shared crazy stories about this old hitter Senior who Ivey used to have eating out of her hands.

"Anyways," Ivey said, "let's get back to The Hanged Man. Relationship-wise, you're at a crossroads. There's no easier way to say it babygirl. There's no reason to freak out though, just take some time to think about the small little clues you've been getting that you need to change your game up. Don't ignore the signs life always sends us, baby."

"What signs?" asked Morgan, looking like Ivey just exposed her.

Immediately, Ivey switched up on her acting like the

conversation never happened.

"Do you want jambalaya or fried shrimp for dinner, lil' girl?" asked Ivey with a small smirk on her face.

"Huh? You tell me Ivey," Morgan spouted sarcastically, "Hell, you know everything else about me!"

—————

CHAPTER 24

—————

Across town at the same time, Chase was shopping online for the latest Chloe bag on Johnny Boy's MacBook. The two of them had to start moving their lil' "honeycomb hideouts" to different parts around the city, knowing John's wife was on alert after the last incident.

"Oh! I'm loving this one right here. Yassssssssssss honeyyyy! Hmmm? Wonder if they have it in black," said Chase excitedly before clicking the checkout icon.

"I know his credit card info is already saved on here, so let me drop this in my shopping cart and pur-chase it while we wait for his Cialis to kick in! Yassssssss! Of course, speedy delivery is required," the fabulous Chase whispered devilishly under her breath.

(((((((Her hotline bling)))))

Nick: Chase, where mi pum pum, gal?

Chase: Jamaican Nick! How are you bud-die?

Nick: I–N–I good. Where you rest? I want' come over dere."

Chase: Play the game how I say play it or not at all. Until next time. Toodles!!

"Oh, Johnny Boy, hurry up with your simple self," she shouted, "Or, should I strike up old faithful again?"

—

Call Chase cold. Call Chase calculating. Those closest to her, call her friend. Chase was everyone's best friend in her small circle. For some reason or another, Chase just had "you can trust me" written across her forehead. How wonderful it was to be trusted with everyone's deepest, darkest secrets, but it was also about to land her smack dab in the middle of some pretty petty "nega mess." Peep!

Chase and Monique had been the best of friends since grade school, of course. Chase and Monique's man, Tremaine, had developed a real close connection since the high school newspaper days. Oftentimes, Chase offered Tremaine advice on how to deal with Monique's crazy ways. In addition to that, Chase was Tremaine's best friend, Eric, best friend too. She meshed with Eric during their random sets when they found they shared a similar vibe and understanding of things.

Since Chase was the centerpiece of this circle of friends, she felt partly, if not totally, responsible for the melee which caused two of her friends to lose their jobs, another one who ended up in the ICU, and how she wound up at this abortion clinic.

—

Her son Kareem was with his grandmother for the night, probably making cupcakes and licking the bowl clean afterwards. Her husband was working late. Dani refused to spend her free night in the house, so she drove way out in the county to a movie theater where no one would see her. She just wanted to be left alone yet entertained. As she moved throughout the parking lot slowly looking for an empty space, she stopped when she spotted her husband's truck.

Dani knew her husband's SUV was far too big to rock back and forth from some slight movement. She stopped her car in front of his, so he couldn't just pull out all sudden. Then, she walked up beside the truck's cab. She pressed her left ear against the rear door on the passenger's side. Her heart dropped when she heard the moans and groans of passion and heat.

With her palms sweaty, she bent down next to the SUV and cleverly pulled up the flashlight app on her smartphone. She took a few minutes to gather herself then stood up quickly, shining the light through the side of the cab's window. She'd caught him, red handed with his hand in the cookie jar, literally. There he was, her first and only love, the father to their infant son, being rode like a bucking bronco by her best friend Yolanda from her job.

Many painstaking emotions ransacked her mind, body, and soul. Sadly, it wasn't even her high beaming flashlight that disrupted them, but the heart wrenching wails she let out that finally broke their passionate rhythms. The bright lights showed the sudden panic of their faces while she banged on the glass and continuously screamed loud and hysterically.

After drawing more than enough attention from moviegoers on their way home, she summed up some piece of mind, walked back to her car, slumped down in the seat for a second banging the steering wheel with her hands. Seconds later, she cranked up her car a sped off like a bat outta hell.

Now, the truth was crystal clear to Dani and her husband. Because of the awkwardness of this situation, Harold saw and heard her frustrations, and on top of that, he also knew his own. Maybe, this is the reason he decided not to get out of the truck, or say a calming word to his exasperated and embarrassed wife? Perhaps, in his mind, he was protecting her co-worker and himself from potential harm. Nevertheless, the husband and the mistress watched mischievously from the truck's window as his scorned wife sped away crazily out of the theater's parking lot. The blinding combination of the darkness of the night and the tears swelling in Dani's eye sockets caused her to miss the huge pothole ten feet in front of her.

She was driving about 50 miles an hour when her front end quickly plunged into the vicious hole and popped right back out. The sudden, blunt impact from the pothole proved to be too much for her small sedan. The shock caused her to lose control of the wheel for a minute, but she somehow navigated the car to the right shoulder.

Coincidentally, it tore up the bottom of her front end and blew out the front tire on the passenger side. She began to cry hysterically. All of this seemed like it was too much for one person to bear on any given night. Frantic, upset, and alone, she refused to call her husband. Normally, she would call her co-worker Yolanda during these moments. Not because she could fix the tire, but she had a brother who owned a tow truck company and a body shop.

Yet, at this point, she didn't want to ask another man for a damned thing. Plus, the last time Yolanda brother helped her out of a situation like this, he wanted more than a few dollars as payment. Besides, she figured she'd witnessed enough folks changing the tires on her car that she could do it her damn self.

So, she jumped out angrily, armed with nothing but her pride and prejudice towards the male species. She grabbed the jack from her trunk. Her car was sitting on an angle heading down a hill, yet that wouldn't stop her now. She nestled the jack under the car with only the lights from beside the interstate providing some vision. Her eyes were still teary, her emotions at an apex, but she found assurance after she started to crank the jack and the car started to rise.

"That's right I don't need no damn man for nothing, no-thing!" she told herself. Her elation kept her from seeing that the downward direction of the car made the jack tilt slowly. She returned to the trunk to scurry around for the other necessities. The weight of her leaning against the car trying to reach the other jack and some gloves caused the car to tilt even more.

After obtaining the tools she so desperately needed, she moved toward the front of the car again. While surveying how everything was holding up on the front end, she clumsily grabbed the side of the car and leaned forward, causing the jack to leap and shoot violently towards her face. The clattering sounds of the metal breaking itself free caused her to close her eyes and cover her face, but to no avail, the heavy metal jack struck her across her neck and the side of her face terrifically and knocked her out-cold on the side of the highway. She lay there helplessly in a pool of blood.

CHAPTER 25

"You'd rather waste her time pretending."

"Please!" said Daquan. "If I would have known Keisha was being true to me then I would have been another type of man for her. I would have been straight up with her from the beginning, instead of assuming she was like all of the others."

"What makes you think she's not like the others?" insisted Morgan.

She continued, "You don't know what your gal be doing for real, for real. Mane, you have done more sticking and moving, and you still want to stick and move, so why waste time trying to be in a relationship? You ain't built for that life, mane. And neither am I! The only difference between you and me is I know I'm not ready. You'd rather waste her time pretending."

"How are you going to tell me what I'm prepared for? You don't even believe in nothing. Nothing! You're a cold hearted, uncaring individual and proud of it. So, yeah, save the relationship advice, Miss Morgan," he shouted.

"Oh, so now you're in your feelings huh, nega?" Morgan said with a sly demeaning chuckle.

"I don' ruffled your feathers now, huh?" she added.

"Nah, what blows me is, you take my sharing stuff with you as opportunities to take shots at me. But you don't want me to put you in a category of no kind. Like you're free to do as you please and you expect some new random guy or an old random to just be sitting there waiting on you after you get through doing whatever you feel like doing?"

"In fact, you're just like most unavailable females..." he started to say before she cut him off quickly.

"Whoa!!! You brought your chaos to me!" Morgan offered offensively.

"No! I shared what I was going through to you as my friend. Not to be judged by you, but to be heard," Daquan interjected.

Silence spoke.

"You know the other day I realized that of all my friends and their weak, stupid relationships, I'm the only one close to being happy," Daquan spoke softly and assuredly.

"Ha-ha," Morgan scoffed, "well good for you, mane. Big freakin' kudos to you and that naive gal you with."

"Oh really? Well, I'll have you know the only naive girl in a relationship, right here, right now, is you—Morgan?" Daqaun responded emphatically.

"Mane, how do you figure that? I do not deal with love." she scoffed.

"How are you so arrogant and so naive at the same damn time? How? You're so blind it sickens me sometimes," Daquan stated passionately.

"Mane, you are really blowing my high and pissing me off,"

she announced angrily.

"You really don't see it, huh?" asked Daquan.

"Really don't see..." Morgan asked cluelessly.

"I'm in love with you. There—I said it. I'm in love with you, Morgan!" Daquan screamed.

Her frown dissipated. Her anger left. Utter cluelessness was all over her right now. Sadly, all she could come up with at that moment was, "Daquan, you know I don't do that mushy stuff mane. You know that! Mane, why did you have to say that. Y ou're ruining a good friendship with this bull, mane!"

Daquan turned to her and belted out again, "Morgan, LOVE doesn't give a f*** whether you feel like it, act like it, talk about it, or you care for it; Love just cares for you anyway. And I care about you, and I always have."

"Mane, I gotta another nega on my line about some money, so let me call you back," said Morgan quickly exiting the conversation.

———

Morgan Facetimes Que immediately.

"Que, What's good with you and your dude Daquan lately?" asked Morgan.

"As far as what?" asked Que.

"I mean it's like we useta play Pimp, Tonk, Spades, Dominoes, and shoot pool all the time. Now, since his lil' girlfriend showed out that day, he been scarce like fresh water in Flint?" inquired Morgan.

"Wait! Why...are you...so worried about Daquan, Shawty? That's off limits for real, for real," Que stamped, staring her down cold.

"Mane, first, you ain't my damn daddy. Second, why are you counting my boy toys anyways. And third, who do you think you're talking to like that, Que? I mean, we cool bruh, but believe me, this is business way before it's personal at this point. So, if I have a problem with the potency of your products, I'll get at you, but otherwise, mind yours bruh." Morgan said ripping him apart.

"Remember you asked me the question, right? Right? I don't mix business with pleasure, so if it's like that then you don't have to get with me, Shawty." Que secured her.

"So, it's the friendship or the product, because you can't do both. Plus, he's one of my closest brothers who you know has a crazy ass girlfriend always on his trail. Doing that would be a real violation, Morgan."

"Again, why...do you...care so much?" Morgan asked disgruntledly.

"You act like you and him sticking wood in each other!?" said Morgan disrespectfully.

"Maybe, we are...Hold up...Wait...took that too far," Que laughed out loud. "But seriously, I know you and I know him, and it's already becoming a concern and y'all ain't even on each other like that yet. Right?"

(Silence spoke for a moment)

"Right Morgan?" Que inquired again.

"I mean we been texting strong, for real, for real, and I would've been cool and respectful about us, but...but...his broad tried to flex on me, and I can't let that go down like that," Morgan chuckled.

"So basically, you're saying that this liking Daquan or whatever ain't even about him, but it's on some get back to his girl."

"News Flash!! It's always about the other women with a female. There is nothing a man can really offer us other than money. Oh and sex which is wack most of the time because usually women have that one guy with that perfect wood that got us turned out in the beginning and we always long for it no matter who were with, but it is what it is though," stated Morgan..

All Que could do was shake his head at her commentary.

"Anyways! Let it be known that Morgan will never go out like some basic weak, dull broad because the nega I like is letting his girl keep his nuts in her purse. Believe that?" Morgan reiterated.

"Listen Que, just step back, and let me raise him up a little because she has him on 'son-status' and I know deep down he doesn't like that," she remarked.

"True as that may seem," Que interjected, "you still have enough dudes in your face all the time, Shawty! So, stop it."

"But why though? Stop what? And—Why? Why, Que? Why huh?" she asked crazily.

"Oh, I think I get it," she paused briefly, "I guess the real issue is why I'm into him and not you, huh Que? "

"Girl...Git dafuq outta here!" Que responded.

"Nah! Seriously, nega. What's good with your feelings for me, Que?" Morgan asked.

"Let it breathe, babygirl," Que answered. "We've been friends and business partners going on 10 years now, and I ain't about to let you put me on blast like that. I ain't sweatin' you, lil' girl!"

Morgan responded, "That was not my question. So back to what I said originally...am I giving your boy Daquan too much attention and neglecting you, Mister Quincy?"

"And, for the second time, I ain't answering that, period," Que responded, "you would know what it is, if it was, Morgan, believe me."

"...how many times has your stank mood helped y'all's relationship?"

"Monique, what in the hell is going on?" Ms. Bey said anxiously.

"Thank you so much for coming down here, Miss Bey. I ain't have anyone else to call—that I—trust—like you, ya know?"

"Girl! Why are you all cut and bruised up, Monique? And where the hell is Chase right now?"

"Hmm—things got a little crazy at my job today, Miss Bey."

"At your job?" Miss Bey asked.

"Well, actually in the parking garage to be more specific!" Monique said.

"Lil' girl, didn't I teach y'all years ago, 'no drama around your what?'"

"Our J-O-B! I know Miss Bey. No drama and thangs around your money train!" Monique answered.

"So—what happened?" Miss Bey asked. "And start from the beginning."

"Miss Bey, first—let me say—I...Excuse me—my jaw is still hurting..." Monique said whimpering.

"And it's badly swollen by the way," said Ms. Bey, "but anyway, go 'head."

"I love Chase. She has been my heart since sixth grade."

"BUT," Miss Bey asked.

But—she acts like life's some damn ratchet reality show or something," Monique said angrily.

"Okay, Monique, let's pretend I'm clueless. What does all that supposed to mean, exactly?" said Miss Bey slowly getting more frustrated.

Monique said, "Chase spends too much time watching me live my life instead of living her own life. Hell, its real things happening and she's trying to play every side of the game. Sooner or later, you must be loyal to someone. Everyone should not be equal to everyone else!"

"Okay, okay. Now, what does that have to do with ME having to take off work to pick you and your best friend up from the ER in the middle of the afternoon?" Miss Bey shouted.

"So—Chase gave me a ride to work this morning and we got into this riff about some relationship things as always..."

(Monique proceeds to tell the story from earlier...)

"Look, I love you Nique and I'm always going to listen to you, cry with you, and be strong for you, BUT do you notice every time you tell me about a good situation turned sour with Tremaine it's your random manic mood swings that caused the ruckus," Chase asked Monique.

"It ain't no damn mood swings for nothing; that dummy always does something that makes me so mad and I can't help it," Monique said firing back at Chase.

"Okay. Look at it this way, how many times has your stank mood helped y'all's relationship? How many times has Tremaine changed what he does that makes you mad in the first place? How many times has your funky attitude made him grow closer to you? Don't worry I'll wait?" Chase said.

"Oh, that's how we're going? Well, at least I can show and prove that I care about mine! Can you at least make a choice? John? Rashid? I don't just sit there and take it or just cheat on them like you do, Chase!"

Chase reacted, "Oh bird please stop chirping! You need to stop it; you cheat. Maybe not in action, but how many times have you boned Eric in your mind while you were riding Tremaine?"

"Oh lord...mmm mmm mmm wait that's different," Monique said, rubbing up and down her thighs sensually, "that dark piece of chocolate there is just dreamy, honey, you hear me?"

"Yeah, whatever," Chase responded, "that boy don't want you Nique. Plus, he's best friends with your man!! Something is seriously wrong with you."

"Chase aka The Fabulous Chase as you like to call yourself," Monique retorted, "don't you always tell me, babygirl, you only live once? Huh? Isn't that your favorite line?"

"See, that's totally different," Chase said matter of factly.

"No, it only applies when it's you, huh? Self-righteous dark chocolate, bird!!" Monique said with a huge smile on her face.

"Forget you, hoe!" Chase said, laughing hysterically. "Don't take it there now!"

"No! No! No! Damn that, Chase, if I only live once, then let me live then...once!" Monique said with a sassy little attitude.

"... laid out in a pool of blood on the side of the road ..."

Random Jamal had been humping Morgan for a good hour. All you could hear was his grunts, his headboard, and the sweat dripping off his face and splashing onto hers.

"Eww. Aight mane, seriously, go get you a towel or something, you're sweating all over my face nah," an agitated Morgan screamed.

"Shawty, shut up please, I'm working here!" Jamal responded. "Maybe if you would do more than barely spread your legs, or part your lips to say something motivational to a brother, this session could have been over, maybe even legendary," he jabbed back.

"Mane, for real, for real, ain't nothing legendary about you but your wallet. By the way, you should be happy I'm giving you some of this buttercream in the first place," scoffed Morgan. "Why ain't you just getting it from your ole lady, anyway? What is it? She can't cut it no mo' or is it that you're rhythm-less or your stroke game weak," Morgan chided him in a nasty tone.

He fired back viciously, "Keep my folks name outta your mouth, Shawty. I don't disrespect your main dude, so don't disrespect mine."

Frustrated and disgusted, Morgan closed her eyes and

blocked out her present reality. Mentally, she traveled back to being happy with someone else. Don't get it twisted, Morgan rocked with Jamal. He was a "nice" guy who gifted her crazily and on the regular, so she always thought why not? Not because she had committed a cardinal sin of love, ending up with an undesirable. Sooner or later, all "gamers" feel this way.

One week had passed, the walls were closing in on Morgan. Randoms had crowded her life and everything seemed redundant. It was obvious she needed to make some serious decisions.

———

Morgan received a text from a former, favorite Random while riding with her new random Daquan.

(Text thread)

Ramel: Where is he now?

Morgan: Right here...

Ramel: Doing what?

Morgan: He's sitting right next to me driving

Ramel: WTH? Is he slow or something? Not paying attention to you.

Morgan: No! He has no reason to suspect me of doing anything different than what I tell him I do...

Ramel: Oh really...

Morgan: ?

Ramel: Whatever baby...

Morgan: Whatever?????

Ramel: It doesn't matter...Less 4 him, More 4 me

Morgan: Smh

Ramel: So, r u ready to break free of him yet?

Morgan: NO, Y?

Ramel: Then, y r u entertaining me???

Morgan: You're still cool people's mane

Ramel: Yeah! And ...

Morgan: Then, that's what it is ...

Ramel: Oh????

Morgan: Oh what?

Ramel: We'll, I don't need any more friends... Sorry

Morgan: Then that's sucks for you man and it's too late ...

Ramel: Meaning?

Morgan: We already are friends

Ramel: Nah boo...I need more...Plus, what about the dude sitting next to you...

Morgan: What about the girl in your house? Oops! I mean your roommate.

Ramel: Look, I'm giving you what he can't right? Half of what I'm giving you is more than 100% of what he brings to the table, right?

Morgan: I need you but maybe not in the way you are thinking though

Ramel: Oh, how is that?

(Morgan pauses for a few moments to take a call from her Auntie Ivey)

Morgan: Yeah, I do need you in my life, but it ain't like you're making it seem...

Ramel: How the hell is it then? We are so perfect together when I'm spending and sending for you when I'm on the road but now you don't need me like that? Get on gone girl....

Morgan: WTF mane, stop texting me then...

Ramel: Okay, be that way. It's dead Shawty

"Hello!!!" Daquan chimed in Morgan's direction. Morgan jumped, looking shocked. "Oh yes baby, are you alright?" She barely could keep her attention on him as she constantly checked to see if the Ramel had texted her back yet.

Realizing that her mind and attention was far from him, Daquan retreated internally to process the whereabouts of her mind. While she focused on her phone, Daquan started to focus on her thoughts searching for clues, "So, what's up? In a deep convo huh?"

Morgan answered clumsily, "What do you..."

Just then her cell vibrated, and she stopped mid-sentence, "Umm...umm...what do you uh...mean baby?" Stuck in between answering the phone and responding to her man, she grunted loudly, "AHHH!!!!"

At that moment, Daquan realized her dilemma and snatched the phone from her hands before she got a chance to read the text. He held the phone with his left hand and steered with the other, just to test her reaction.

Morgan yelled, "What the hell? I bet you better give me my damn phone!"

Daquan yelled back, "I bet you better give me some damn attention."

"Give it," Morgan screamed.

Morgan was desperate; desperate to keep what she had with Daquan going strong and desperate to keep her "human woodpecker" Ramel on deck too. She worked well in this setting usually, but Ramel's text and Daquan pressing her about these anonymous texts was becoming too much.

"I bet you better give me my damned phone cuz you sure as hell don't pay the bill for it," Morgan screamed again.

Meanwhile, Ramel finally sent her another text making the phone vibrate while it's in the Daquan hands.

"Oh!" He threw her cell back in her lap, "Your baby is texting you back cuz its vibrating again. I guess that's why you keep the ringtone off, aye?"

While her phone was still vibrating in her lap, she looked at Daquan with fire in her eyes for disrespecting her by throwing some inanimate object in her direction, but her heart was yearning for the Ramel's reply. Trying not to look so suspicious, Morgan picked up the phone without looking at it. The suspense was eating her alive.

Still game-tight, Morgan flipped the script easily. "You know what...if it will make you feel better," placing the phone in his lap, "here you keep it."

"Ha-ha! Oh really?" Daquan laughed. "You know your phone is locked now!?"

"Oh, I'll unlock it for you sweetie," she said nastily, "if that's going to make your insecure, jealous ass feel better."

Now, the energy had shifted. He knew if he asked her to unlock her phone and reveal the messages, then he would appear bitch-like. But he also knew if it was something to be found then he had her caught and red-handed. Their eyes met. Their heart rates sped up. Both were faking like it doesn't make a difference either way. If Daquan decided to give her the phone back, then she'd dodge exposure and her secrets would remain safe. If he'd asked her to open her messages, then the cat is out of the bag and she'd have to fall way back.

Suddenly, Daquan's cell phone rung. It's Que's brother's sidepiece, Janna. She is shouting, hysterically, and nothing she is saying is making sense. He shouted for her to calm down and tell him what was going on.

"I'm with Jason, and we just drove up on Dani laid out in a pool of blood on the side of the road," Janna said.

"What the hell?" Daquan yelled.

Morgan asked, "What...what, baby?"

Daquan asked Janna to try and calm down. "Now, where are y'all now, babygirl?"

"We are right down the street from the AMC Theatre on the West Side," Janna replied.

Daquan hit a U-turn right quick, darting across a four-lane highway and speeding towards the interstate.

"What's wrong?" Morgan asked again.

"Janna, Que's brother's sidepiece, said they just found Dani laying in a pool of blood next to her car. Looks like she was trying to change her flat tire or something and something went terribly wrong!" Daquan shared with an anxious Morgan.

"Where dey at now?" Morgan asked desperately. Daquan said that Janna and her crew were following the ambulance back to Providence.

CHAPTER 28

Random Games amongst Men

Basketball on Sunday afternoons was a like religious pastime for Tremaine, Eric, and several other guys from the old neighborhood. Tremaine's mentor owned a gym and trusted him to bring the right kind of guys around to play pickup games for three to four hours, lock up, and head home without incident. On this given Sunday though, the other guys were running late, so Eric and Tremaine had some random time to build.

Tremaine asked, "So E, how's that new job coming along at the glass house?"

"Everything's love my brother. Easy work, easy money!"

"True. I'm glad my baby got you on, up there. You know Monique runs thangs in the 'glass house'," Tremaine bragged.

Tremaine continued patting himself on the back saying, "I know it's some Jazzyfatnastees up in there, too. Aye! Don't lie, Bro, I know the females are plenteous up in that piece."

"Yea I hear you, but that ain't why I'm there, man. I'm working on my plan to be a better man, yaknow?"

Tremaine responded, "True indeed. But why not get your money and some honey, Yafeelme? Just stay out of my honey pot, Pooh Bear!"

Tremaine joked, making both laugh, but it also made Eric feel some type of way. Eric knew the real deal with Tremaine's wifey, Monique, along with her friend Chase. "Let's just say this way Tremaine, if there was more honey being offered to me at this point, then I'd doubt that I could handle it, yafeelme? So, I'm good believe me."

——

After watching Dani suffer so severely sprawled out across that hospital bed, Daquan and Morgan decided to squash the petty argument. Daquan had learned that every relationship, whether secretive or out in the open, needed some climate control. Knowing what to say and when to say it.

One day later, Daquan waited for Chaotic Keisha to come home so he could get her car and ride out. Daquan laid the game down flat on Morgan, so when he came for that cookie, she couldn't front on him at all. As Daquan whispered to Morgan, their secretive conversation was surprisingly interrupted when Keisha walked in the door from work.

"Hey baby," Keisha greeted him warmly.

"Hey!" Daquan reacted nervously, "you scared a brother barging in the door like that."

He clumsily grabbed all her bags and his plan was to dash into the other room to cut off the phone, but sensing something strange, Keisha asked, "No kiss today?"

"Oh yeah," Daquan stopped, gave her a quick peck on the cheek, and quickly made his way into their bedroom.

By then, a deathly silence had fallen over the line because he didn't have time to cleverly end the call with his baby Morgan without going noticed. Thoughts of panic filled his mind, "Damn! I hope Morgan hung up the line before she heard that exchange of words," knowing that Morgan wouldn't want to hear him kissing her nemesis.

Slickly, while Keisha laid down her keys and purse, he canceled the call.

"Damn!" Daquan thought to himself.

"Damn I left my other phone in the car," Keisha said. So she retreated downstairs to retrieve her phone from the car and check the mail.

Kicking himself for allowing such a messed-up situation to occur in the first place, Daquan quickly called back Morgan to plead his weak case and say how he didn't mean for all of this to happen!

(Phone rings over and over)

Masking the hurt and shame, Morgan chided, "Let me call you back later on tonight."

"If that's how you want to play this baby," Daquan asked, certain that he'd get more of an emotional reaction from her.

Morgan replied, "I told you I would call you back since you hung up on me."

"Damn," he repeated, "if you say so."

"Alright then," Morgan ended the convo sarcastically.

CHAPTER 29

"... And grabbed his left bicep ..."

He could barely hold onto his keys to get in the door. Now, whether it was the pouring rain making his hands slippery or Morgan's slippery body all over him, no one knows, but Stone had a time trying to fit his key in that lock.

Totally attuned into him, Morgan had his neck in a cobra clutch, sucking, biting, kissing, and caressing. Her hands covered all sides of his tall chocolate frame like rushing waters after a dam break. Finally, he twisted the key to the right, cracked the door handle, and the weight of their bodies popped the door open so forcefully 'til it slammed up against the wall beside it. Drenched clothes hit the floor, as the lightning castd shadows of their silhouette every time it flashed.

It was the moment they had waited on for months and finally they were into it. Stumbling through the house like two snakes intertwined, they tripped over the loveseat and onto the floor. Finally, Morgan's body slumped from the passion, knowingly, totally submitting herself to him. His demeanor was cold and vengeful. He was ready to pay her back for all the emotional hiccups she caused them in the past year. Her mind was on this moment, and her eyes were carefully fixed on him as she happily spread eagle, so his champion wand had plenty of wiggle room. He rolled up her soaked–n–wet white sundress.

Of course, she didn't have a speck of undergarments, so she had been tantalizing him since the rain started. Stone stopped and took a long look at her small petite frame and aching furry temptress. He quickly set up on his knees to retrieve his sword and seemed to leap inside of her from anticipation. As soon as his mushroom entered the gateway of her temple, he grunted loudly and grabbed his left bicep. His body went limp and he fell over her left leg, lifeless and breathless.

"Stone! Stone!!!! Stone!!!!! Baby, no!!!!!!! Wake up love. God No!!!! Wake up baby!!!" she screamed as she reached for her cell phone.

—

"Mane, please don't let this mane die," an erratic Morgan told Shania.

"What happened though, Morg?" Shania asked.

"Shania, we had the most intense, explosive episode ever and then..." Morgan shared sadly.

"Oh, my Gawd!!!! Wait! He passed out while y'all were just ...getting...into it?"

"Yep! And why does this type of stuff always happen to me? I don't deserve this...at all!" Morgan pleaded.

(The doctor walked up to them)

"Are you all here for Rob Stone?" he asked.

"Yes! Mane, please tell me he's okay...please!" Morgan

begged.

"Ma'am, I regret to inform you that he did not make it," the doctor expressed somberly.

"NOOOOO!!!!" Morgan shouted hitting the floor face first. Shania sat beside her and listened to her wailing. She rubbed her back and shed a few tears with her. "I am so sorry Morgan," she said. After five minutes or so, they sat up, Indian style, on the dirty ER floor. "So, doctor what happened to him exactly? He's young, healthy, and strong!"

The doctor responded, "Miss Morgan, he seemingly had sniffed a large amount of cocaine and combined it with a few sexual stimulant pills, and although young and relatively healthy, his heart could not take it. I hate saying this to you, Miss Morgan, but everyone has a limit. Do you want to report this to the proper authorities? Perhaps, the guy who sold this to him will be prosecuted."

"Mane, what? Please, have a good day, doctor." Morgan responded.

"Let me say something to you though, that man was my heart. I wouldn't know anything about love had it not been for him, and you trying to judge him on his drug use. You ain't a Black man in America muthafuggah. As a matter of fact, F*** you. It's your fault because you should've saved him!"

Morgan and Shania moved to the outside of the ER. As they stood, Morgan wiped her eyes and pulled out her phone. "Hello! Heyyyy Ramel, meet me at Providence Hospital!" Morgan told her long-time Random.

"Wait! What? I thought you loved Stone, Morgan?" Shania asked. "How are you going to just move on to the next one like it ain't nothing?"

Morgan responded, "He died okay...But remember now... how many times you had to be a tissue-passer because he did some dumbness? How many times have you helped wipe the tears from my eyes that he caused me? Huh? Huh?"

"Girl please!" Shania replied with her lip poked out.

"Nah, nah Shania! Answer me?" Morgan asked raising her voice.

"I mean more than a few times girl, but that works both ways too," said Shania. "Think about us women though, these guys ain't treating us worth spit. They pass us around like we're just a bunch a fish in a ridiculously small pond. And all of us allow this, in one way or another. There are simply different types of bait that trap us, the bulge of his wallet, the bulge in his pants, or both," Shania continued.

Morgan shook her head and chuckled like they were some sad cases. "Yeah, my Auntie hit me with some craziness the other day. You know she reads those tarot cards and follows the stars and all that?"

"Yeah I know how she do!" Shania answered.

Morgan continued, "She was like looking through our club pics on social networks the other day and was 'baby y'all look so good, all made up and dressed to the nines, but y'all so sad.'"

"SAD!" Shania repeated. "What does she mean by that? We be turnt all the way up."

"Nah, she was like, 'look at this picture, now look into your eyes, babygirl.' She was like 'focus on your smile. There's sadness in your soul,'" Morgan expressed.

"Tell her, Nah, it was that liquor. Hahaha," Shania chuckled.

"But Ivey said that's a part of it too. Because you know I went there, too. So he was like 'your smile doesn't meet your eyes, Morgan.'"

Shania cried out, "What!!?? Ivey tripping now!"

So, Morgan pulled out several random pics that she had discussed with Ivey and Shania got real, real quiet for a minute.

Then Shania said, "We just doing what we do. It ain't that deep?"

And as shallow as Morgan can be at times, this time she was like "Nope. It ain't that deep for real, for real, BUT we ain't that happy either."

CHAPTER 30

"That's what fear will do baby. It paralyzes you ..."

Monique continued to pour her soul out to Miss Bey. No more pride. No more "I'm grown too" into angles. Just a wayward child similarly trusting her innermost thoughts to her loving mentor.

"I've been playing Tremaine for a long while now. I've done things right in front of him. I mean, you could barely call it sneaking around. He never says a word, Miss Bey, and wouldn't dare try to check me on anything."

Well...it sounds like Mr. Tremaine followed his right mind today, mm?

"Miss Bey, I was terrified. All I heard was his tires screeching around those tight corners of that parking garage! He whipped around that corner and there we were...totally exposed!"

"What the Hell do you mean by—WE?" Miss Bey stopped her mid-sentence.

"I was sitting on the hood of his best friend Eric's ride. My legs were spread. Eric was standing, well, he was grinding on me while whispering something in my ear. The sound of his tires and his screaming brakes made both of us pause and look in that direction. My jaws just dropped Miss Bey."

"Umph!!! I bet your jaws dropped. Knees got wobbly. Heart starting pumping too," Miss Bey added.

"Tremaine looked us right in our eyes, put his car in park, took a few pulls from his cigarette or a blunt or something, and just sat there for an awkward second or two.

With his hands raised in the air and already coppin' pleas, Eric quickly separated from me. I quickly hopped my trifling-self off the car's hood and tried to straighten my weave. We had been made, fully exposed, and I was trying to think of a way to flip this back on Tremaine or sacrifice Eric, yaknow?

"'What am I seeing here?" shouted Tremaine, pulling out his strap from under his seat. "Yo E, I know, I know, I know, that YOU KNOW better than to bun-up with my gal, mane!?" Tremaine asked.

"Tremaine cocked his 9mm and rapidly moved towards us. 'Wait!   So, you've been my man-50 grand-from third grade ....how you...how you....going to press up with my baby mother?'"

"Put the Glock down, T! Stop waving that because if it goes off, you're headed to the pen - PERIOD," a suddenly arrogant Eric said, "You know what this is - and what it ain't! All that other stuff is you and Monique's business, not mine. Real talk!"

"Talk to this man, Monique," Eric continued.

—

"I froze Miss Bey!" Monique admitted. "I just stood there silently, somewhat stupidly because my sundress was caught up in my boy shorts, so when I looked down my thighs were exposed almost up to my crotch."

"That's what fear will do baby. It paralyzes you" Miss Bey said.

——

"Nah, Nah! Damn dat, E! I've been knowing something strange was going on. I felt it. Damn that, I know it now! It's done! You should've known not to finagle with the mother of my kids. Every nega knows not to mess with your bruh's baby mother. Every nega knows its certain folks you do not touch in your bruh's family: his mama, his sisters, his baby mother, and his children. They are off limits. Always off limits. G Code, nega," Tremaine explained.

Just as the tension got really muddy, Chase screeched around the corner. She was coming to pick me up, but surprisingly, she ran into some drama she saw unfolding months ago.

Chase slammed on breaks and hoped out shouting, "Whoa! Whoa! Nega, what in da...!!! Tremaine, Tremaine, why do you have that 9 at your man's face like that? And why are all these tears streaming down your face. I ain't never seen you boo-hoo -EVER!"

Chase looks towards me next and gives me the nastiest side-eye. "And bish, why is your skirt stuck all in between and betwixt your damn legs like that?"

Then, Chase turned in Eric's direction, his demeanor was still as cold and thoughtless as ever, but Chase led into him too. "Sun, Sun! No, you didn't mane? Not here, not now!"

"Monique, why did you bring him down here?" Chase asked, walking up on Tremaine putting herself between the gun and Eric and me. She softly placed her hands over Tremaine's heart and felt it jumping out of his chest. Then, she whispered something in his ear."

Tremaine remained emotionless, never dropping his weapon. I was still frozen with fear, taking little light breaths. Eric, like a character in a gangster flick, was cold as ice.

Right then, Chase, who had everyone's trust, attempted to diffuse the situation. She said firmly, "Eric, sweetheart, go back to work." She pointed at Tremaine, "Don't even think about squeezing one off."

Then she turned towards me and said, 'Fix yourself up and go sit in my car, now."

As I walked, I gave Tremaine the softest most innocent face I could, like the preacher's daughter who'd just got caught sexing in the church.

Then, Chase addressed Tremaine again, "Let me get this off of you, baby."

"Nah, nah! Hell nah, damn dat, Chase," Tremaine yelled back, "This nega is always sitting in the cut, scoping people out, calculating thangs, but he didn't calculate this one though. Chase, you know Monique helped get this nega this damned job. At first, I thought he was just being ambitious, just trying to get his money straight. Nah, this nega was trying to get with her the whole damn time. I smelled it. That's why I rolled up with that Glock cocked because I knew something was up with Monique's sneaky ass. All this time they are spending together: breakfast runs, lunch dates, smoke breaks, and whatnot. My baby mother though. She pushed to get this dude the damned job and now she posted up with him, letting him grind on the place where our daughter was born. Tongue down her throat and whatnot. Nah, nah, Chase, I can't let that slide. Hell Nah!"

"What!!! What!!!" Chase stammered, "What...You're just going to...going to...Uhhh!" Then, Chase called earl all over Tremaine's shoes.

"Chase, what the?!" a startled Tremaine asked.

———

"Miss Bey when I saw my friend in jeopardy I just reacted," Monique said.

"See, I'm convinced you've got to be crazy. Your man has a loaded weapon. He's pissy mad with you because he just caught you with his best friend, and your fickle behind is running towards him trying to help the friend who's trying to keep him away from you," Miss Bey replied with a puzzled look on her face.

"Anyways - carry on?" Miss Bey said.

———

So, I hop out of Chase's car and rush to her aid. As soon as I got within his range, Tremaine pimp slaps me with his gun. All I remember was blacking out for a second.

When I came too, I was covered in blood and as you can tell it ruined my new cute 'fit I'd just bought last week. Chase was sprawled out close to me, and somehow Tremaine had got a hold of Eric and was beating the living dawg poo out of him. Eric started to look like Nino brown laying on the trash pile in New Jack City.

Just then several white men walked off the elevator and saw the mayhem and called security, who were off duty cops. Within five minutes, they brought the chaos and rage to a close.

—

"See—Miss Bey—all of this is Chase's fault. If she'd just learn to shut her friggin' mouth sometimes and stop being so two faced, we wouldn't even be in this predicament, yaknow?" asked Monique

"Monique baby, no one is judging you, but didn't Chase save you," Miss Bey said, "I mean that is what it sounds like. AND ...if you hadn't been well, I will leave that alone because you're a woman dealing with all kind of Randoms but still. Get up and go back there and see about her and I'm heading back to work. We're testing today. Here's my card, call an Uber on me or I'll meet y'all back down here after school."

"Oh, my Gawd, Miss Bey!"

"What now lil' girl?" Miss Bey replied.

"Even after all of this! You still love us?" Monique asked.

"Baby, you all still have so many more mistakes to make do you understand me? Just keep on living..." she said over her shoulder heading out the sliding doors of the ER. For over an hour or so, her babies had total access to their motherly figure; something each one of them lacked in their personal lives.

———

Once I reached home, I walked and thought, "Lord, I don't have a clue how to help my babies now. They've really screwed things all up in their lives. Hell, I don't have a clue how to help myself. I feel like you turned your back on me when you took my parents, but here I am stuck here, and I know you've brought these youngens to me for a reason. Give me some direction?"

Just then the thought came to me, "get back into church," but I'd left there amidst so much scandal. So, a mere 15 months later, I waltzed back into the same Zion Methodist church still incredibly attractive and confident externally, but hollow internally. Pastor Thomas preached an inspiring sermon about staying connecting to God through the rough times. I had a wonderful fellowship despite those who still snickered pointed at me and judged me profusely. After the service ended, I made my way to the altar to shake the pastor's hand and right before I reached the Pastor, the First Lady cut in front of me.

"Why are you here?" she inquired. I replied cleverly, "I did not come for you, or your drama, or even your husband. I came to find out why I'm cursed...and...and why the Most High thinks I'm unworthy of someone to love."

CHAPTER 31

Suddenly, she cried out, "Mane, F*** love. F*** relationships. F*** sex. F*** being high to deal with him. F*** getting high to enjoy sex with him. F*** everything that got to do with him! F*** these dumb asses cursing and blowing their horns at me. I am in the way. I'm in everyone's way. He say I stayed in his way too. Now, he's totally out of my way forever. Love and drugs, drugs and love—what a f***ing combination."

"Young lady, let's talk about this!" the officer shouted in her direction feeling the tension reaching its height. She'd reached the brink of her sanity, no more tolerance, no more compassion, so his voice fell on deaf ears. Slowly sobbing, like someone off that Promethazine, she looked through her phone again, and she waited. The officer waited. The *News* 7 chopper waited. The thousands behind her waited. Still, no response from anyone, she scooted closer to the edge.

"Wait!!!" the officer screamed. With no more time to think, he rushed her sensing the end was near. Hearing his footsteps scampering towards her quickly, she turned to the officer with tears streaming down her face and said, "I'd rather be with him!"

She leaped off the high railing.

———

The last conversation that Morgan and Shania had at the hospital when Stone was pronounced dead started her into a weird tailspin. A tailspin that led her to try to leap to her death from Old Dred Bridge. It seemed the random relationships didn't offer enough stability to sustain her.

Her Auntie Ivey always suggested to her, "that the game can have you riding so high, so-so high, totally unattached from anyone or anything, but sooner or later, you must find some place to set your feet."

She laid in that hospital bed in the mental ward for over six months. She studied herself, meaning she took time to take apart every relationship she'd had, from family to men to women, and discovered it's more important to find out what the "self" wants without becoming selfish or self-centered. Her counselor Chad Bryant told her each day in rehab, "Be more selfless in the future, you'll get so much more from everyone in your life."

—

Two months after her bestie Morgan was released, Dani's brain trauma was over with no visible damage in the future. The wires from her jaws had been removed, and she was as talkative as ever. After recovery, she was frightened to learn that her best friend from elementary school, Morgan, had attempted to take her own life.

Unlike so many others who abandoned and judged Morgan, Dani moved her best friend into her house, and they began again. Crazily, Dani helped Morgan get her swag back when their entire lives, Morgan always had the juice, and Dani was the lame duck. Not anymore, Dani was back, body stacked, and her paper had just gotten fat from her divorce settlement. She was happily, legally disconnected from the "cheating bastard who boned someone in a movie parking lot," so it was only right she took her girl Morgan on an all-inclusive vacay to Montego Bay, Jamaica.

(*Pilots charged the passengers, "We are starting our descent onto the beautiful island of Jamaica and we want to extend a warm, welcome to you all choosing to fly with us today. Please, buckle up your seatbelts and prepare for arrival. Again, welcome to Jamaica, mon!!!")*

"Dannielle, my belle," Morgan said excitedly, "do you see this beautiful ass water, girl? I can smell the ganja, the fruit, and the water way up here!"

"Yaknow! But, damn that, show me where I can find Dexter St. Jock with Dark bronzed body and long locks?" Dani said, with her newly single and ready to mingle self.

"Oh! Oh! Oh! So, you're about that life now, huh?" Morgan asked, ending her question with a big "'FINALLY'"!

"Yasssssss hunneyyyy!" Dani said smiling before an intense look covered her face, "I am ready to hit the reset button on my love life and start a new journey.

EPILOGUE

An oldie but goodie song once proclaimed, "I want to know what love is—And I want you to show me!" Here I am old enough, wise enough, experienced enough, desperate enough TO KNOW WHAT LOVE IS! I do not. Plus, the way I've taught my students to know and understand love was bulls*** too because I nearly lost one for a random relationships gone haywire.

Let me stop. I shouldn't say that because art is the grandest way to express love and share it with the world, but love ain't no joke y'all.

We're all seeking love in this story.

Dani sees love through the eyes of an 80-year. She's a throwback girlfriend who came to me naive and wearing her heart on her sleeve, but she leaves this after having an awakening.

Chase is the digital girl, the social media dolly that lives for likes and the world of make believe where you can find love in a superficial way without getting deep into the passions and emotions.

Morgan walked through my doors a rebel desiring to only use and manipulate love for personal gain and ended up receiving the biggest smack of all from love.

Now, as for me, I wanted love and felt I deserved love, but this year revealed how shallow I'd lived. These babies coupled with my grief and a need to compete with every other women caused me to lose my job, my respect, and my sense of self.

Now, here I am after all I've learned still seeking love because now I realize with love, you can always start over.